The

Mayan Magician's Kiss

The Water Priestess Trilogy

The Awakening

By
Abby Isadora Haydon

Book and Cover Design
by
RamaJon, Bikeapelli Press

Cover Credit Jeff Zavala, ZGraphix Productions

One Blade Press books are available for order through
Ingram Press Catalogues

Abby Isadora Haydon

Visit my website at www. spiritualguidance.com

Printed in the United States of America

First Printing: December 2014

Published by One Blade Press

ISBN: 978-0-9831980-3-1
Ebook ISBN: 978-0-9831980-4-8

Dedication

To

RamaJon and Tom Bird

The dynamic duo that got me writing again

Table Of Contents

Introduction

This work of fantasy is infused with a great deal of reality. Even though the story line is fiction, much of the knowledge of indigenous cultures that permeates its pages has their basis in actual myths and legends. The story's antagonist, the vile magician Ixma, was created from a real Mayan folk tale. The legend relates that a witch from Uxmal birthed a son through magic. He became feared as well as revered. Together the two built the Pyramid of the Magician that still stands in the ruins of this once flourishing city.

The potions that are used in the story to go back and forth from the Mayan Underworld are also part of the history of Mesoamerican cultures. The early tribes of the Olmec and the Toltec brought these traditions of drug use to their cultures. They used hallucinogenic mushrooms and cactus as the main ingredient for these drinks. These concoctions were used for ceremonial purposes, for the most part. They were given to victims that were about to be sacrificed. The Aztecs perfected the use of these herbs through their extreme need to sacrifice people to their gods. The Mayan adapted the use of sacrifice and the potions that made their offerings passive. The drugs caused those who were about to lose their lives to appear calm, even smiling. This made the waiting crowds feel that they sacrificed themselves willingly to the gods.

1

The information in the story about Mayan astrology is also true. I have written two books revolving around Mayan astrology. The references to the heroine's Mayan astrology sign is used to validate her destiny. Throughout the book she demonstrates the true essence of her Mayan astrology sign. Morgan becomes the resplendent warrior that is within her potential according to Mayan astrology. Morsels of knowledge about the Mayan calendar system appear throughout the book. The Wayub days are thought to be unlucky. Retreating to a dark home when the old year ends and the new one begins is a tradition that, along with the Mayan astrology, is used by the Maya of today.

The Mayan fire ceremony is discussed twice in the manuscript. The procedures for making and performing the Mayan fire offerings are factual and still used by the living Maya. The fire ceremony has become the main way that the Maya of today make offerings to their gods. These ceremonies are done on Solstice and Equinox days as well special days that honor different gods and goddesses. I describe the way the fire is constructed and how it is used. I had the good fortune to spend a short time working with a Mayan shaman showed me how to do an authentic Mayan fire ceremony.

Along with information about the Maya, I have shared knowledge that I have gleaned as a psychic and healer. My sojourn in Sedona, Arizona has exposed me to many spiritual, metaphysical concepts that I relate through the book. My experience with intuition and the ways that it manifests to us is expressed as a growing synchronicity between the heroine and her love interest. My knowledge of past life regression, that l use in Sedona as a healing modality, is explored in detail in this novel. I also share my perspective on the difference between the concepts of dark and pure evil. I share my idea that the dark energy of the planet has specific functions that are necessary to continue life as we know it. I also relate my knowledge of the ways that communication with the living as well as the dead can take place during the dream or meditation state.

Finally, the material shared about the goddesses that play critical roles in the story is comprised of actual myths and real occurrences. The Mayan goddess of the moon, prophecy and childbirth, Ix Chel, does have the remains of a great temple on the island of Cozumel. The legends of The Morrighan are based upon ancient folk tales. One story of The Morrighan claims that she would appear to soldiers the night before a battle. She could be seen washing the bloody clothes of those who would die the next day. The information about the Virgin of Guadalupe comes from written accounts of her presence and the miracles she performed in Mexico in the 1500's. The cape imprinted with her likeness does hang in the church of Teyepec.

I hope that I help those who read this book to be open to the energy of the Divine Feminine. The goddess frequency of this planet is alive and blossoming. As more people open to the power of the goddess, the planet will come into balance and receive that healing that it needs and desires.

It is my hope that The Mayan Magician's Kiss will transport you to a world where women use their power to live the life embodied within them.

From Here to Eternity

Morgan was treading cautiously through a series of underground hallways. Each one seemed to open up into the next. The walls were made of chiseled stone. They were light grey in color and were rough to the touch. The floor of the passageway was made of tight fitting, slippery stones. She could barely see in the faint light that was provided by torches spaced along the corridor. The lack of light made it possible to only see a few feet in front of her. The air in the walkway was moist and heavy with the smell of mold. There was also the lingering, sweet hint of incense that Morgan felt had remained from long ago. Morgan was almost overwhelmed by the dankness of a place that must have been hidden from the daylight for many centuries. As she walked along the corridors she could see that there were symbols painted on the walls as well as pictures of people in elaborate head dresses. All of the artwork had been drawn with terra cotta, white and black paints. The designs on the walls looked like that had been done recently. All the details of the frescos seemed intact. The paintings on the walls reminded Morgan of Egyptian hieroglyphs. Yet they were not the well-defined symbols of the ancient Middle Eastern culture that were familiar to Morgan. As she walked, Morgan sensed that these symbols were for protection and also for manifestation. She did not know what it meant, but she felt the power emanating from the design.

Morgan's slow, cautious pace made her feel like she was in a maze that might never end. She felt that she could not go back the way she had come. Even though fear was mounting within her, she knew that she couldn't go backwards. Finally the hallway emptied into a chamber that felt to Morgan as if it had been used as a ceremonial room. She could see a stone table that she sensed was an altar on the far side of the space. It was brighter in this room. There were many torches and candles around the place. She was able to see objects on the altar. There were candles, crystals, feathers and many other items that Morgan did not recognize.

As she got closer to the platform, she could make out a black dagger that was the center piece of the altar. She also sensed that she needed to be on guard. She started to tip toe very quietly to the altar. She felt the blade was beckoning to her. Her fascination for the artifact was more than mere curiosity. Morgan actually felt that she was being pulled to the stone pedestal that was about four feet tall. She felt compelled to retrieve the knife from its resting place. As she came closer to the stone table, she sensed that it was used for many types of ceremonies. When she was a little more than an arm's length from the altar, a man suddenly jumped out from a doorway on the left. He had body paint covering his whole form. The white markings on his muscular body gave the impression of a skeleton. His dark brown skin peeked out from under the white markings that had been carefully drawn upon his body. His face was entirely white. His eyes were circled in black. He was menacing to say the least. He made a loud shout and thrust a spear toward her. The spear was black with a ring of red feathers at the tip.

Morgan screamed and then woke up.

The reality that she was on a tour bus zooming through the Yucatan peninsula of Mexico came back into her consciousness. Morgan De Armond was awake and traveling swiftly on a thread of highway in the middle of the Meso American rainforest. All that she could see were the tops of the trees that appeared to be packed in tighter then sardines in a can.

"Morgan, are you alright?" she heard a young, high pitched voice as she opened her eyes. Hovering over her was a teenager who had adopted Morgan during the sighting seeing trips. Morgan got the impression that Heather was a lovely young girl, blossoming into womanhood. Her mothering instincts were kicking in, and Morgan appreciated the nurturing.

"Yes. I am ok. I just had a strange dream. I really appreciate your concern, but don't worry about me.' The young girl bent over Morgan, gave her a hug, and then went back to her seat.

"Wow" Morgan thought to herself. "That was a strange nightmare. I guess it came from all the Mayan ruins that we have been seeing for the last few days. I wish that I hadn't forgotten the relaxation tea that Esmeralda had packed for me. I haven't had any nightmares since I started taking it. Oh, why did I leave it in the hotel two days ago? Now I must be feeling the effects of not using it." Morgan stared out the window and watched the trees of the rainforest whizz by. "The dampness of the ocean air must have gotten into my dream," Morgan thought pensively. Yes, she was beginning to have the nightmares again. The theme was always the same. Someone or something was always chasing her. Or else someone would show up and start to attack her. She had started to have these dreams a few weeks before she had shown Gerard the pictures that had been taken by a private investigator. It was her dreams that made her want to find out if Gerard was cheating on her in the first place. When her billionaire husband had seen the photos of himself and his Vale ski instructor in a hot tub, he went into a rage.

A couple of days after that, Gerard had started the divorce proceedings. He did not want to talk to her. He had no desire to work this out or get over it together. It was then that Morgan realized that the dream life she had been living was now evaporating before her eyes. In less than a week, Esmeralda, one of the maids, had given Morgan the tea bags to calm her nerves.

"Take this tea at night, Senora. It will help you to sleep and it will relax you." Morgan had gratefully sipped the tea every night. It had helped her to sleep. The tea had put her into a very relaxed, almost numb state.

The last three months had left Morgan feeling abandoned and alone. Suddenly everything that she had gotten used to was soon to be taken away. She had been ushered off to the Malibu house to await the outcome of the divorce. The last time the statuesque beauty, with a yard of jet black hair and deep green eyes, saw her spouse; he was on the other side of the cold, glass conference table of the lawyer's office.

As the divorce proceedings were coming to an end, just ten days ago, Morgan's lawyers had suggested that she go to a language school in Mexico for Christmas. "You won't feel so lonely if you are not in the same setting. The holidays are so hard the first year," they had said. Morgan hoped that they were right. She had loved to oversee the decorating for the winter celebrations at the main mansion in Montreal. She had never celebrated Christmas growing up. Her mother and grandmother, her only relatives, celebrated the Winter Solstice. The three of them only did somber ceremonies for holidays.

"New setting, New experiences, New life" Morgan repeated to herself as she watched the trees go by. Her Yoga teacher, a kindly old Indian man named Shuru, had told her to make these phrases her new mantras. She had many private lessons during her time as a member of the Gerard De Armond family. Qigong, shamanic breath work, Yoga, horseback riding and tennis were the activities that filled her days. That had been her life for nine years. Now a new life had to begin. By the Summer Solstice she would be a single woman again.

Morgan had acquired a fondness for the members of her class. There were twenty nine other women who had decided to make the journey to Southern

Mexico in search of cultural enrichment. She was the only one of the class that was getting a divorce. The rest of the women were Midwestern housewives and Beverly Hills teens that were very into bling.

Morgan had been interested in the list of events that were provided by the tour company that was separate from the school. There was going to be a full schedule of tours to Mayan ruins, snorkeling and an enactment of the Mayan handball game. Losing her tea had had left Morgan feeling tense and apprehensive. Her joy at taking this new journey had evaporated. Yet Morgan wanted to be a good sport. She didn't want the gravity of her life situation to weigh heavy upon her sister tourists. Yet she could not help herself now.

Tears started to stream down her face as her hand groped inside her bag for the picture of her soon-to-be ex-husband. Next Morgan went through what she had named her picture ritual. From deep within her oversized Indian print tote bag, Morgan withdrew the picture of Gerard. He was holding a fish he had caught on his boat, Mirage. She held out the picture at arm's length, then pressed it to her chest and let out a big, long sigh. After a few moments of quiet sadness, she put the picture back in the bag. She was not over Gerard. She was still in love with him. She had hoped to work with him to change his straying ways. His response was to stay away from her completely.

As Morgan gazed out the window at the passing trees, she realized that her feelings of desperation were enormous. Everyone had deserted her. She couldn't be angry at her grandmother, Molly. She had died two years before she had met Gerard. Morgan's mother was another story. On Morgan's wedding day, her mother's message was: "You have made your choice. Now you will bring either great glory or great shame to our house." Her mother did not attend the wedding. When Morgan tried to get in touch with her, she found that her mother had left town with no mention of where she was going. At the time, Morgan was in love and didn't feel the loss. Now it was a festering wound in her heart. Morgan, who had just turned thirty six months ago, had no one to help her through this challenge.

"In a few minutes, we will be turning off the main highway. We will be in the little village of Boca Negra. The group will have dinner there and then watch the Mayan fire Ceremony that is done on the Winter Solstice," the tour guide announced. This notification caused all the women to start shifting around in their seats. They were getting ready to disembark from the bus.

Morgan looked around the bus. She could see that all of the women were preparing to leave. The bus was now slowing down, ready to turn off the main road. For some reason, unknown to her conscious mind, Morgan felt frozen to her seat. She did not want to get up and leave.

Morgan noticed the contrast between the blanket of complacency that had been surrounding her recently to what she was experiencing now. "I have

11

felt so anesthetized since the divorce started. Maybe my intuition is resurfacing," she thought. Morgan did have the gift of clairvoyance. It ran in the family. Her mother made their meager living by giving psychic readings in a few of the Santa Monica and West Hollywood metaphysical bookshops. Morgan thought back to those times and chuckled. "I could never get over on my Mom. It was like she had a computer screen in her head that told her everything I was thinking." Another big sigh came from deep within Morgan. "I wish she would come back into my life."

The bus was now changing gears. It was starting the arduous task of going over the pot-holed dirt road to the evening's destination. All of the students were being tossed back and forth in their seats. The well preserved vehicle began the final phase of the journey to Boca Negra. Morgan decided to compose herself and get organized too. She sat up and straightened out her blue gauze yoga shirt and pants. The loose fitting top had a big OM symbol that covered her small but perky breasts. She dug into her purse and found a comb that she used to straighten out her tangled hair.

As the bus rounded a curve in the dirt road, the ocean with its gently breaking waves came into view. As soon as Morgan saw the waves coming into the nearby beach, she started to cry. The scene reminded her of her rides with her beloved horse, Raven.

"Oh I miss Raven so. Riding him always made me feel so much better," she said to herself as she sobbed loudly. While she was going through the legalities of the divorce, she had ridden Raven, Gerard's thoroughbred black stallion, every day. She had felt as if she was now living in a whirlwind. Raven helped her get to the calm of the eye of the hurricane. It had been almost a week since she had left Malibu, a very long week without her only friend. "I don't even know if I will be able to keep him. It will be so hard to go on if I lose him," she realized and started to sob even more.

Her sister classmates had expressed their concern throughout the trip. One motherly woman from the Midwest had told her yesterday, "Just let it all out dear. You do have a lot to cry about." Indeed she did. The life she had known for the last nine years was definitely over.

She had started her first quarter as an art history major at Santa Monica Junior College when she met Gerard. She had been playing in the waves, talking to the ocean, in front of his Malibu estate. Suddenly, the six foot, blond Adonis with a French accent was bouncing around in the waves with her. From then on, her life had been right out of the TV show "How to Marry a Billionaire." The heir to a French wine export business had been very generous. He had been so taken with Morgan that he built a stable for her so that they could keep some of the family horses at the Malibu house. After she had ridden Raven the first time, she knew that she could never ride any other horse. She felt as if he had always been her horse.

"I am sorry to be so emotional," she said in apology to the group.

"Don't worry honey. Some of us have been where you are now," a matronly woman chimed out from the front of the bus.

"Thanks," Morgan replied. She found some used facial tissue in her bag and used it to blow her nose.

The bus was now coming to a stop in the cove where Boca Negra awaited them. To say that Boca Negra was a village was kind, but untrue. There was nothing at Boca Negra except three brightly colored buildings. One was yellow, one green and one pink. The buildings looked like squares with doors. All the structures had rebar sticking up from the corners. Strung between the buildings, were rows of paper snowflakes of pastel colors. In front of the grouping of buildings was a line of picnic tables, covered with plastic, flowered tablecloths.

When the bus came to a stop, all the women were ready to get off. Morgan was still feeling glued to her seat. She was overtaken by a nameless fear that was preventing her from getting up. The tour guide came up to her seat, hoping to pry Morgan out of it.

"It is time to leave the bus, senora. You will eat dinner, watch the Mayan fire dancer and you will feel better."

Morgan nodded in agreement to the tour guide. With several deep breaths, she gathered her fortitude and stood up.

"Very good. Right this way." The tour guide was watching her closely as she escorted Morgan to the bus door.

Morgan still felt apprehension and unexplained dread as she stepped off the bus and walked into the village of Boca Negra.

As the class approached the tables, they were greeted by a line of Mexican women in traditional garb. They were wearing white blouses with large colored flowers that were tucked into knee length, solid color skirts. They were all wearing sandals with tire soles. All of the women, except for one, were middle aged and beyond pleasingly plump. There was one that caught Morgan's attention. She was tall and had a body that would put Pamela Anderson to shame. Her glistening black hair was pulled back in a bun, like all of the other women. This only made her splendor more obvious. She had large cow eyes and full, plump lips. Striking was the word that came into Morgan's mind as she walked by her to find a seat at the end of the line of picnic tables.

Morgan felt the weight of all her sadness came down upon her as she sank into the picnic bench. The dream had been disturbing. She felt a dark, ominous cloud had settled over her.

"Maybe some beer will help lighten my mood," she thought. "I just want to forget all about my life with Gerard and have some fun tonight." Her eyes followed the pitchers of the golden liquid that were set down on all the tables. The women were also carrying platters of shredded chicken and taco fixings. Some of the women brought covered baskets of tortillas that gave off an inviting aroma of corn and stone.

"Ladies, dinner is served," the tour guide announced. The women knew that it was their signal to eat. The majority of the women attacked the platters with gusto, but Morgan just focused on filling her beer glass. As the first glass went down smoothly, Morgan began to relax. She decided to have another glass of beer before making decisions about food. Halfway through her second glass, she decided to contemplate the taco potential. Morgan got a plate and made herself a lettuce taco of avocado, tomatoes and cilantro.

"Almost a salad," she chuckled to herself. Morgan spent the next twenty minutes chatting with the other students and eating her version of a taco. As Morgan emptied her third glass, the tour guide made another announcement.

"It is time to go down to the fire pit to take part in the Mayan Winter Solstice Fire Ceremony. When you are done, please file down the little path to the right of the tables and it will take you to the fire pit."

Most of the women took this as their cue to get leave the taco feast and saunter over toward the fire pit. The blazing fire could be seen from the eating area. Morgan was now feeling the desire for group bonding, and went with the other students on the little path that led toward the ocean. As Morgan merged with the line, she was feeling festive. Three glasses of beer on a fairly empty stomach was acting as a great mood enhancer. She actually started giggling as she walked down the path.

"I am glad to see you feeling better, Morgan. You have been through an awful lot lately."

"Thanks, Heather," Morgan answered. "I guess it just takes time and a positive attitude. I am doing my best, but sometimes it just over whelms me. I have been told it is good to get my feelings out. I wish it was more enjoyable!" Morgan gave the young girl's hand a squeeze as they approached the blazing fire.

"That is a big fire." Morgan stated as she found a seat next to Heather on the rocks that made a half circle around the pit. The women were arranging themselves around the fire when the tour guide started to speak.

"We are now going to have a fire ceremony that is similar to the ones that were done during the time of the ancient Maya. You will each get a little ball of Copal. It is a tree resin that has been used for thousands of years by the Maya in all of their ceremonies. It is said to purify the atmosphere and act as an offering. At the height of the Mayan empire,

17

bloodletting was also used as a form of offering to the gods. The King and Queen of each large city did their bloodletting in public. The King pulled a knotted cord through the fore skin of his penis. The queen pulled the sacrificial rope through her bottom lip. The blood fell onto a cloth and the offerings of the royal family were then given to the fire. Aren't you glad that you only have to throw the ball of Copal into the fire?" The tour guide laughed at her joke and the rest of the group did the same. While she was talking, one of the serving women came around to each student. She gestured for each one to take a piece of Copal from the woven bowel that she carried. When the woman approached Morgan, she thrust the small, natural fiber basket in front of her. Morgan could see the tiny, dark balls in the container. She closed her eyes and picked one. When all of the women had a piece of Copal, the tour guide spoke again.

"Now it is time for you to throw your Copal into the fire. Please make a line. It is good to speak your intentions or wishes as you throw the tree resin into the flames." The tour guide was the first to throw a ball of Copal into the blaze. She stood in front of the fire and was silent for a moment as she mentally repeated her prayer and pressed the ball to her heart. Then the tour guide tossed the ball into the flames. She turned to the group, pointed at Morgan, and indicated that she should be the first of the group to take part in the ceremony.

Morgan stood up and with the small sphere pressed between her two hands in the Hindu prayer position, she approached the fire. When she was close to the bonfire, she stood for a moment and then started to say her prayer out loud. "I just want to ask the powers that be for help in starting my life over. I want to use my potential, enjoy life, and find true love." With that Morgan threw the blackish, dry tree sap into the fire. The rest of the group applauded as Morgan sat down. She smiled at everyone and gave Heather a hug. She felt thankful that the group appreciated her efforts.

As the rest of the group started to go through offering their prayers to the fire, the extremely charismatic serving woman approached Morgan with a tray of ceramic mug. As she got closer, Morgan could see that there were symbols imbedded upon them. The women smiled at Morgan and handed her a steaming cup.

"This is the traditional Christmas drink, Atole," the woman stated as she handed Morgan the mug. Morgan noticed that she had a thick accent. The woman's speech sounded different from the other Hispanic speakers she had encountered on the trip.

Morgan looked at the thick concoction with hesitancy. She was about to hand the mug back to the woman, making the international sign of "No thank you." by shaking her head.

The woman stepped closer to Morgan and whispered loudly, "It has lot of rum in it."

Morgan winked at the woman again and then downed the drink in one pass. She was feeling good and she wanted to keep that mood going. She put the empty mug back on the serving woman's tray. The woman let out a small sigh as she took the mug and then continued upon her rounds.

Morgan was feeling content and peaceful in front of the fire. Her eyes came to rest upon the fire and she felt that she was going into a light trance. Morgan began to see images in the flames. She could make out a black figure there. Then the image seemed to turn into a long, dark stick. She could see two other shapes that reminded Morgan of people. One was bigger than the other, yet the small figure seemed to be chasing the larger one around. The larger figure was using the stick to keep the smaller image at bay. Morgan was enthralled with the images. It was like watching a silent movie. Her grandmother had taught her to see images in a still bowl of water, but Morgan had never seen pictures in the flames.

After all of the women had thrown their Copal into the fire, the group heard a loud shout that definitely came from a male. Morgan and the rest of the guests soon realized that this was the announcement that the entertainment was now underway.

The women next saw the source of the shout: a spectacular, well-built man suddenly leaped out from behind an outcropping of rocks. He was a bit short by US standards but he was an excellent specimen of masculinity. The performer had on a skimpy Mayan costume. He was wearing a headpiece that seemed to be fashioned from a Jaguar's head. The rest of his attire consisted of a crotch piece that was made from a Jaguar's tail. He had symbols drawn on his mocha colored skin. He was twirling a flaming baton as he started to strut around the fire. The audience could see that he was enjoying prancing around the blaze, in front of the gathering of responsive women. Morgan was delighted to see this magnificent man. Every muscle in his body was very well defined. The light of the fire made it easy to see his firm, abdominal 'six pack' as well as his well-developed thighs and upper arms. Morgan liked looking at a guy that obviously worked out. In short, the man was beyond superb; he was a sexual magnet that easily aroused all the women in the audience.

Morgan, Heather and the rest of the young women began to let out with some cat calls and hoots. They all seemed to be enjoying the amusement immensely. The man was looking at Morgan more than the other women as he paraded around the fire. His gyrations reminded her of Elvis. He was thoroughly mesmerizing. His sexuality came across forcefully to Morgan as it did to the entire group of woman. It was as if they were at a bachelorette party and he was the male stripper.

After a few festive minutes, Morgan began to feel a subtle nausea in her stomach. Soon it started to distract her. She realized that she needed to use the restroom. Even though Morgan was hesitant to leave the party, she knew that she needed to listen to her body. When Morgan stood up to look for the restroom, the enigmatic serving woman came up to her and quickly indicated the way to the building that said Restroom. Morgan nodded and thanked her. She found it a bit challenging to make her way to the restroom. Trudging through the sand and the intoxicants of the evening made the walk of a few hundred feet seem like a grueling mission.

When Morgan entered the lavatory, she was taken aback by the resemblance that the facility had to her high school's restrooms. There were several stalls and a trough-like sink opposite the stalls. Morgan was able to make it inside the stall just as the urge to make offerings to the toilet gods came upon her. She made several offerings before she felt her stomach calm down.

After the waves of release had subsided, Morgan felt that it was time to get out of the stall and wash her face. She slowly made her way to the sink. She had just turned on the water and started to splash it on her face when she heard a familiar shout. She turned her head to look toward the door, and the incredibly brawny, profoundly sensual Mayan dancer was standing at the entrance to the restroom. He was smiling and beckoning her to follow him.

Morgan responded with "All right!" She wiped the water off her face with a nearby paper towel and turned to face him.

When he saw that she was looking directly at him, he started making gestures that indicated to Morgan that she should follow him. Then he disappeared from the doorway. Morgan started to follow him, but she found that it was not easy to walk. Indeed, Morgan felt that she had lead weight tied to her feet. The desire to follow him suddenly took over her body. As quickly as she could, she got to the doorway. Once there, she found that he was standing at a distance, near the water, signifying that she should follow him.

Morgan did not need a green light to go for her goal. "I bet the lawyers set this up for me. They must have gotten me the deluxe package. This hunky guy must be the Mayan desert for the evening!" she laughed to herself. She was ready to follow him. She had felt so rejected when the divorce started. Now, Morgan was in the mood for meaningless, hot, sweaty and obviously wet sex. "Like from Here to Eternity" she chuckled to herself as she envisioned a night of lovemaking on the beach.

The Mayan dancer was being a bit elusive. He kept running away. Morgan kept following. She saw the bonfire out of the corner of her eye as she pursued her diversion for the evening. The exotic, erotic muscle man darted behind a rocky wall and out of sight. "He must be waiting at the perfect place for a tryst," she thought as she made her way over the wet sand. When she turned the corner, she found what she was seeking. The Mayan dancer was waiting for her. His arms were open, beckoning her to come to him. As she walked toward the man who was way beyond inviting, she had to step over some small boulders. As she stepped over one, she was able to make out that the stones were arranged in a circle.

When both her feet where in the stone ring, she instantly saw a dark crimson light erupt from its center. The blood red radiance quickly spread to the full area of the circle. Next other sensations started to engulf her. She got a sense of extreme compression. It felt as if her body was being pressed flat. Morgan could not open her eyes to see what was happening. She felt force coming from front to back and on the sides of her body as well. She could not move. She also heard a horrible screeching noise, which sounded like thousands of little kids screaming at the top of their voices. This occurrence lasted for what seemed like a short time.

Suddenly, all the noise and pressure stopped. She felt as if she had taken a ride in a bizarre drainage pipe that had now emptied her out into some unfamiliar ocean. Her senses told her that she was floating. Morgan realized that she could breathe easily in this water-like situation into which she had plummeted.

Even though there was little light, she could make out that she was hovering in a rectangular, grassy area that was bordered by two stone walls. She was not in water, even though the sensation of floating was the only sense that was familiar. She was suspended right above a design that looked like an equilateral cross.

Before she could take in the new surroundings in greater detail, her body started to drift through the air. While she was moving she could see an array of colored lights in the distance. She could also see several buildings with people all around them. The buildings reminded her of the Mayan ruins that she had seen that day. She did not feel as if she had been to this place before. It appeared as if the people were watching a light show of some sort.

"The floating thing is happening again," she thought as she was being pulled toward a large building, past the colored lights. It was very tall, and looked like a pyramid. She was soon sailing over the tops of the heads of a large group of people, watching the light display, on her way to the pyramid. In her blissful state, Morgan felt that she wanted to get the attention of the people below her, to say hello. She started waving her hand in a small gesture, like the Rose Parade queen. When that didn't seem to get their attention, she made bigger motions, moving her arms back and forth in a semi-circle over her head. She still got no response from the group below. Then she started yelling. No one looked up as she floated over their heads. The reality became clear after a bit: "No one can see me or hear me." Yes, she was sailing above a crowd of spectators and no one could perceive her. She didn't want to have this next thought, but somehow it snuck in: "What is happening to me???"

It only took a few moments for Morgan to find out. She stopped and lingered at the base of the pyramid for a few moments. Then her assent to the top started. She slowly went above all the narrow steps that led her up to the top of the ancient structure. She thought that it must have been about a thousand feet tall. Her feet remained a few inches from the ground when she reached the roof. The top of the pyramid was flat. As Morgan stood suspended in the air, at the pinnacle of this ancient structure, she saw the lights from a nearby town in the distance. She could see that beyond the light of the small village were the lights of a harbor. The illumination made a semi-circle off in the distance.

Before she could even take a moment to contemplate this situation, the exotic, primal, sexy-as-hell Mayan dancer magically appeared in front of her, about 20 feet away. The amazing Mayan entertainer was thrusting his hips, as if to give Morgan a preview of what was in store for her. She started to giggle. "I am beginning to enjoy this trip." Before her hovered an extremely tempting fellow. His arms were open to receive her and his captivating smile and hand gestures beckoned to her. Then she felt like she was on the airport conveyor belt. The conveyor belt was taking her right into his arms.

Suddenly, Morgan felt like being coy and playful. As she came closer to the hunky dancer, she laughed and floated up in the air so that her feet were level to his eyes. This caused him to laugh. He also looked a bit astounded that she could move by herself, but he did not seem to be concerned. He floated up to meet her, and they were again eye to eye, about ten feet apart.

Morgan smiled and reached for her tote bag that had stayed with her during the ride in the shrieking drainage pipe. The strap was smashing down one of her breasts. She now adjusted the strap so that her breasts stood out more. Morgan was definitely being aroused. She even started tossing her thick, black mane of hair around to entice him.

Mr. Mayan man was enjoying this display. He let out a big laugh and flashed his enchanting smile. She looked at him with "come hither" eyes and backed up a foot. This little cat and mouse game that Morgan was enjoying tremendously was also entertaining the dancer. He started mimicking her facial gestures and suggestive stares. In a few moments, they were both laughing as the glow of sexual promise filled Morgan's body.

"It looks like this guy will make me feel REAL good," she thought when he pulled off his Jaguar loin cloth in a very theatrical gesture. The absence of the loin cloth revealed an extremely hefty penis that had already come to attention. Seeing his incredible-looking erection only made Morgan giggle and she responded with a full body squirm of delight. Morgan felt a sexual synchronization start to build between them and she started to move as well. Morgan decided she would do a seductive dance for him as she came within reach of his outstretched arms. "Boy, I am really getting into this" she exclaimed as she felt her body moving in ways that had never before been part of her sexual repertoire.

"I am getting in touch with my inner sex goddess!" she thought as the dancer came close. Then his fingertips touched her shoulders. "Cold!" was her first reaction. His fingers felt as if there was no blood circulating within him to warm his body. "Cold hands, warm heart" she giggled to herself as he drew her closer.

By this time, Morgan had gotten used to the idea that everything about this night was strange and unusual. As his frigid hands started to grasp her shoulders, she felt a very strong heat. It seemed to be coming from her heart area. First, there was heat, and then there was pressure. Morgan looked down at her body and saw that it was encased in a brilliant, glowing emerald sheen. Then, there was a loud noise that reminded her of a sonic boom.

That was all that she could remember. Next she felt that she was being propelled through the air at a tremendous speed. There was no screaming kid noise and no intense pressure. All that her senses perceived was velocity and cold. In what seemed like one0 seconds, she landed on wet sand with a heavy thud. Then she felt waves wash over her.

The Magician Of Uxmal

Concha felt exhausted and worried. She had seen Ixma's fuming face in her dreams last night. She saw his anger that the woman got away. She also saw that his energy was fading quickly. He was not able to suck the life from the tall, thin, dark-haired women from L.A. The botched encounter at the Pyramid of the Magician was costing them both dearly.

She was lying down in the back of her four-door Mercedes sedan while her two lovers took her to the Mayan ruins of Uxmal. "Nothing like this has ever happened before. Ixma will be able to solve this problem." Concha kept repeating these two thoughts in her head. She knew that she couldn't handle this situation herself. She needed to talk to Ixma. "Everything has always gone so smoothly. He will know what to do. After all, he was the great magician of Uxmal." Concha chuckled when she had that last thought. He was a great magician 3,582 years ago. Now, however, the situation was very different. Concha let out a demonic little laugh when she thought about her brother and the state that he was in now.

"What is so funny, mi Amor?" That question came from Enrique, the lover who showed a bit of mental promise. Concha was too weak to sit up and tell him what was so funny. She knew what to say that would make him feel important. "I was thinking of all the fun that we are going to have when we get back to my house."

"Oh, mi Amor, I have been thinking of it too. You are such a wild panther!!"

Concha had a bad feeling about the woman from L.A. before she took the Atole. "She seemed to be different from the others. She was not as inhibited. And so emotional! They said that she cried on the bus all the way from Cancun. Even so, she had some strength in her that allowed her to resist my brother. This one is a curious woman," Concha thought. "Ixma will know how to fix it," she thought. "I have to keep my worries to myself. If the boys know that there is something wrong, it might affect their performance. I don't want that." She ran her tongue over her lips.

The ride from Playa Del Carmen to Uxmal always took a couple of hours. It was hard to rest in that uncomfortable tour guide uniform that she had to wear. Enrique had stolen it from the car of a tour guide. Concha wanted to be prepared in case such a situation should ever arise.

Concha let go of some deep breaths and let herself be lulled into a relaxed state by the hum of the engine of her late model Mercedes. She was very thankful for all she had. She thought of her mother, Katna, and what she had always told her. "Be grateful for all that the gods send you." Now that she was in a half-asleep state of consciousness, Concha's mind started to drift back to the times of her childhood in Uxmal.

The day that her brother was born was a remarkable day, to say the least. Her brother's

30

conception did not begin in the way humans are birthed, for he was not human. Her mother, Katna, had been sitting in ceremony with a group of her friends when she decided to share an idea that had been nagging at her for quite some time. She wanted to tell her friends now. They were in an elevated state of awareness, due to the ceremony they had all just done to welcome in the Mayan week. All the Mayans in Uxmal, at the height of its glory, had to perform a ceremony at the beginning of each new 13 day week.

Many of the women banded together to do the ceremony. It made the energy stronger and fulfilled the obligation to the gods without doing all the work individually to bring it about. They did not want to experience the wrath of the head of their village if they did not participate in a Welcoming of the New Week ceremony. He went to all the homes in his jurisdiction to make sure that the ceremonies were being done and the proper offerings given. He had to make sure that the gods were being honored. If the god that ruled over that week was displeased, it could bring about any type of catastrophe down upon the city. Everyone was forced to pay homage to the gods. Their way of life revolved around making sure that their deities were happy.

Some of the women decided to do their ceremonies at a different friend's house each new week. This time it was at Katna's house. She felt comfortable talking to these women. She wanted their opinion and their help.

"I want to have another child" she said loudly, before any of the women could leave. What she heard from the group was a lot of very loud moans.

"Have the gods made you crazy? Why do want to go through all that again? You barely survived Eba's birth."

"And you are so old that no man who has produced a child would even look at you, no less take you to his bed." Her friend Octa, who was a bit rude and crude by nature, expressed it clearly. The men who went around pollinating the single women in the town had a special name: Chicchanta. These were the men who were said to have the power of the serpent within them. Men had this honor bestowed upon them if they sired healthy children with several women. They were given many benefits from the king of the city and they lived a pampered, comfortable life. They all had apartments in the royal house. Some of them even charged the women trade beads for their services. Most of the Chicchanta only wanted to mate with the attractive women. The King let these men do as they pleased, for he knew that they held the future of the city within them. He desired only the strongest citizens and warriors inhabit his domain. That is why there was so much competition for the attention of the Chicchanta.

"What insanity within you is calling out for another child?" her friend Cibla asked.

"I want someone to help me in my old age. I want to have a male in my family. Then I will feel safe and won't be harassed by anyone." The women all nodded in agreement. It was hard for a single woman to live in Uxmal. The men in the town were always forcing the solitary womenfolk, who had no one to protect them, to do extra work for them. This was a common practice that plagued single females in any Mayan village or city. The husbandless women were always looked down upon. They were pressured to do cleaning, washing and other types of menial labor for the men who had families.

"I am tired of being used by the men of this town to do their dirty work." By that, Katna meant that because she had skill as a midwife and a witch, she was always called upon to get rid of pregnancies that were not wanted. Katna was also forced to do spells that brought harm to others. She hated to do that, particularly to people that she knew. The men in town required her to do their bidding or suffer their wrath.

"You would have to save for years to get one of the male sires at the palace to spend a few minutes in your bed!" One of the women stated jokingly as she looked around for her belongings. The others chimed in until the little hut was vibrating with a loud uproar of laughter.

"No," Katna howled as she was overtaken with amusement. "I have no desire to birth a child the usual way. I want to do it through magic. I wish for a son born of the supernatural. I need a protector. I would like a helper," she said as she sat on the floor of the hut. When she said that, her friends, that were beginning to leave, suddenly looked at each other and sat down. This new idea was interesting to the women. They all had a bit of magical knowledge, but not a great as Katna. They all wanted to know how this could happen. If it worked, maybe some of them would consider it.

"I need to meet with the great witch of Chichen Itza. I have heard from some travelers that she has great powers. If anyone can help me with this, it is her."

"You are going to ask for her help?" Batzke said. "I have heard that she is mean and angry all the time"

"I have to. I don't know of any other witch in this area that can do this type of magic. She is the only one who has ever brought forth a living being from a spell."

"Yes I have heard of her," chimed in Menka. "She birthed a monkey from an egg. It is a big leap from a monkey to a person. Your child could come out with a tail!" All the women laughed at that remark.

"Katna, how do you know that she can do it? It might backfire," a concerned friend added. Even back in the time of the ancient Maya it was common knowledge that magic could easily go wrong.

"I know all of that. I have been thinking of this for a year now. It is time." When the ceremony for eight Batz comes up, I will go to Chichen Itza and ask the witch for the magic to produce a son. "

That was all that was said. Katna turned away from her guests and began putting her dwelling back in order. The women got up and filed out of the little home in silence.

"You are foolish!" one of them said as she left the hut.

Katna's mind was now set. She was going to ask the great witch to give her a son. When Katna went to sleep that night, she prayed to the goddess of childbirth, Ix Chel, and asked her to give her a sign that she could go ahead with this plan. Eight Batz was the most powerful ceremony day in the Mayan tradition. She would go to Chichen Itza and bring many offerings to the witch.

The next day, as she was heading to the market, she heard the cry of a new-born baby making the announcement of its arrival into the world. Katna felt that this was a sign sent from IX Chel. If the baby was a boy, then it would be a very clear that she was mean to continue with her mission. Katna went into the abode on the pretext of giving congratulations over the birth of the baby. She really wanted to see the sex of the child. The proud mother had the baby lying on its back. Katna could see that it was a boy. Katna offered the proper prayers for the new baby, as was her duty as a midwife. She left the residence with a big smile on her face.

When the day came to travel to Chichen Itza for the great ceremony of eight Batz, Katna and her daughter, who later became Concha, set out on the journey.

Concha was very agitated. "Do not aggravate me today," Katna announced as they were making ready to leave. "Just do what I have asked. Then we will have the blessings of the gods, and our goal will be completed. "

Concha shook her head in agreement and went to gather all that they needed to take on their journey. They set out on foot for the great ceremonial center of Chichen Itza. It was the place of the serpent power. It was the place where Kukuhlkan would come to rest when he returned to the Maya. The mother and her child traveled for two days to reach the city. During the first day, it did not rain on their walk. As it was getting dark, Concha was beginning to get worried. She could see the rain clouds gathering. Concha knew that the rain was not far away. The little girl was very nervous. Fortunately, they passed a hut that was abandoned, so they could take refuge there from the rain that followed within less than an hour.

"See, my child, the gods are smiling upon us. They have given us a place to stay for the night." Katna was using her loving tone of voice. It was a tone of voice that Concha rarely heard, but was thankful to hear at that time. It meant that she was not going to get hit tonight. Her mother was not going to take her wrath out upon her. On the contrary, Katna was very pleased at the events of the day. Katna gave Concha a generous portion of food and the child feel asleep quickly.

They only had a few hours rest before Katna awoke her daughter and started to travel again. Her mother gave her some leaves to chew. Katna said that they had come from a witch that often made journeys to the far South where the Pachamama ruled the land. The leaves were precious because they were hard to get. The girl chewed the leaf and suddenly felt like walking. She also felt happy.

There would be many new sights in Chichen Itza. Concha had never been there before. The two arrived at the outskirts of the great Castle of the Serpent as night was beginning to appear. They found a common house, where poor travelers could stay during important ceremony days. Katna bought some of the special foods made in the area for the feast days. When Concha started to eat, she realized how hungry she was. She devoured the Mayan delicacies and was still famished. When she asked her mother for more food, her mother responded with a slap to her head. One of the other travelers took pity on the child and gave her a few small cornmeal cakes. Finally, Concha fell asleep.

The next day, there was a great deal of activity, as there is on any feast day. The travelers were up before dawn. Dawn was the sacred time. It was the time when the Maya did all of their ceremonies. They felt that dawn was the time of power; it was the instant when one could connect with the gods. It was the point in time when all the Mayas, in all parts of the land, would ask for favors of the deities.

Eight Batz was the day to make fresh starts, to create new patterns, to make a new web of life. That is just what Katna wanted to do. Make a new start with a child that she could love: a son. She hurriedly pushed Concha out of the hostel and into the street. They arrived at the main pyramid where the ceremony was about to take place. There were thousands of people there who had gathered at the base of the pyramid to see the king do his bloodletting. As the ritual commenced, many cheered the king on with each knot that he pulled through the foreskin of his penis. When the cord had gone all the way through, and the cloth beneath his body was soaked with blood, the crowd let out a great roar. They were celebrating with the king. They were exhilarated that their ruler had made this sacrifice for them.

Concha, however, was terrified. She saw the blood coming down from the king's body, and she let out a loud shriek. Her mother had to yank her out of the crowd and take her to a deserted alley. Her mother told her to stay in the narrow passage. She would come back for her when the observance was over. For the next hour, Concha sat in the narrow corridor, watching people walk over her to get to the spectacle at the Pyramid of the Serpents. When her mother returned, Concha was sleeping. She was shaken back to wakefulness.

"Get up. We are going to see the witch." The two made their way past the throngs that were going in the other direction, to where the marketplace was. The multitude was ready to celebrate.

Soon they arrived at the house of the illustrious witch of Chichen Itza. Katna was pleased to see that the witch was in attendance. This was a feast day, and the witch was selling potions and other herbs to the visitors from all over the kingdom of the Maya. Katna waited until all the other customers had left. The witch let her gaze rest on the two miserable little people standing in her doorway: a tired, sleepy child and a very anxious mother. At first the witch thought the child was ill, but she soon realized, from the way her mother treated her, that she was just beaten down.

The witch knew of Katna. She also knew there must be something Katna wanted of her that she was not able to do herself. This puzzled and worried the witch. 'What does she crave? Can I give her what she desires?" These were questions that the witch had in her mind as Katna and Concha sat down before her. This was the waiting room, the place where the witch first met with clients. The enchantress was wealthy and had what could be considered a large home by Mayan standards. The witch felt sorry for this girl who had the look of a scared animal. The witch was very perceptive indeed. She would often use her ability to look into the hearts of people who came to her. "I see sadness in the child and desire in the mother."

After they sat down and the witch had given Concha a sweet treat, she turned to Katna and bluntly said, "What do you want. What do you seek from me to do that you cannot do yourself?" Katna turned bright red at this remark. She had never met the witch before, but her remarks only told Katna that she was very powerful indeed.

"I want a child, a son" she stated simply. After the witch heard that, she let out a laugh that would send shivers down the backs of most people. While the witch was calming down, Katna took her response to mean that the witch would help her. "She has not sent me away, so that must mean that she is capable of doing the task," Katna thought to herself joyfully.

After the witch had stopped laughing, she asked, "What do you want to give me in return?" What Katna said surprised even the witch.

"My daughter is all that I have of value for such a difficult task." Concha did not hear this. She had fallen into a deep slumber after she had something in her stomach. They both looked at the sleeping girl. They both knew that it was best if Concha stayed with the witch, even if the witch did not help Katna.

"Done," the witch decreed, and that was all that needed to be said. Katna and Concha spent the next three days with the witch. Concha was content to have a full belly throughout those three days. Her mother had stopped hitting her. The witch of Chichen Itza was being very kind to the child. She gave her small jobs to do around the hut, and Concha felt very good about herself after completing them.

During those three days, Concha watched her mother apprentice with the celebrated sorcerer. Katna was learning to cast a very powerful spell. First, the senior witch had Katna get certain ingredients from the local area. Then she had her put the ingredients in separate baskets. On the last day, the witch went over three times with Katna the order in which to use the ingredients and how to mix them. Everything had to be just right. A very anxious Katna studied the witch intently, trying to remember her every move, her every utterance.

When it was time to leave Chichen Itza, the witch sent Concha to the well to get some water. While Concha was gone, the witch told Katna:"You must bring the child home with you. She has to be there for the birth. Go now. Remember: you must do the ceremony on 13 Ancestors. Do not do it on any other day if you want your son to be a magician."

Katna packed up the precious herbs and tools such as an eagle claw, a Jaguar tooth and bit of a fingernail from the great ruler of the ancient city of Palanque. Katna knew that these ingredients were hard to come by. However, she felt that she had gotten the better of the deal. Her disdain for her daughter was now replaced by her jubilation at the thought of having a son. Katna knew that she had taken her disappointment about Concha out on her. Katna had always wanted a son. She was very distressed when Concha was born. Most people thought that her sadness was from having the baby, not from what sex the baby was.

On the journey home, Katna was very pleased. Elated was a good word. She did not hit Concha anymore. In truth, she had stopped being angry at her and did not take her irritation out upon Concha again. Once they were back in Uxmal, and the days grew closer to 13 Ancestors, Katna started to feel troubled. The weather was hot and humid. The ingredients, such as the herbs, were beginning to mold. Katna did all that she knew to keep the ingredients fresh, but she could smell them fermenting. She did not want to do the ceremony on a different day, yet the next 13 Ancestors was a long time away, and the ingredients would never work then.

The day of 13 Ancestors was a very busy one for Katna. She had to get the biggest egg that she could find. The egg had to be fresh. She went to the market that day, and got an egg that was very big. It was so large, that it was being observed by everyone in Uxmal as they passed by it in the marketplace. When Katna saw the egg, she felt that it was laid just for her and her plan. It was very expensive, about ten times the price of a normal egg. The price did not matter to Katna. "No cost can be spared to get my son," she stated as she carefully walked away with the prized egg. Katna walked home slowly, as to not take a chance of cracking or damaging the egg in any way. When she got to their hut, she placed the egg in the corner of the room that had been prepared for this day with great care.

Then Katna went to work. Concha was sent to Batzke's house to stay out of her mother's way. As

Concha was leaving, a group of women, that she knew to be mother's friends and some other local witches, filed into Katna's little shack. None of the women gathered there knew exactly what was to take place. Only Katna knew, and she was being quiet. She had put herself into a light trance before dawn, and sat waiting for her assistants to arrive.

When they were all seated, Katna told the women of the procedures for the task that was about to be undertaken. She gave a few of the component to each one. She gave different ingredients of the spell to the women who were skilled in using them. She kept a special group of items for the enchantment aside that were hers to use. At exactly the same time, the entire group of women started to chant. They were repeating incantations that they had been taught by Katna just for this occasion. The Copal smoke filled the little dwelling. The intoning and Copal smoke gave the neighbors the idea that something powerful was taking place. They all left the area shortly after the chanting began.

The chanting and ceremony lasted for more than three hours. Concha was at the house of Batzke, who was doing ceremony and prayer by herself. She had special mantras to do and needed to give it all of her attention. She gave Concha some sweet corn meal cakes. The child was soon resting in the arms of slumber.

When all the toning and spell casting had been done for the birthing of Katna's son, she took the ingredients and rubbed them all over the egg. It was covered with a brown, herbal paste. When she was finished, all the women dispersed and Katna decided to take a walk. She had been sitting for too long. She was feeling elated. This was not unusual for being in ceremony all day. She often felt this way when she finished a charm for a couple who wanted a son. Now she would finally have one of her own.

Katna arrived at Batzke's house to find her friend and her daughter fast asleep. Katna scooped Concha up in her arms and took her home. Concha was left to sleep near the large egg covered with the brown herbal mixture.

Concha awoke to shrieks that seemed to come out of a creature from another world. The sounds did not give the impression that they were made by a human being. They were not. They were the reverberations of her brother birthing himself. He was clawing his way out of the egg. Concha wanted to run away, but her mother kept her there. The witch of Chichen Itza had told Katna that Concha must witness her brother's arrival. The trembling child saw her brother emerge from the egg. He was about a foot tall. Within a few moments of freeing himself from the egg shell, he blew up to what was to be his full height: three feet.

In a matter of minutes, Concha was standing next to her brother, who was the same size as her. Instead of being happy, she was horrified. She thought to herself, "Who is this ugly, bloody, screaming creature that stood before her?"

As if to answer her question, Katna came up to her and tried to sooth her. She took her hand, along with a cloth dampened in water, and led her over to her brother. "This is your brother Ixma," she said to the child. Concha started to cry. "I know that this is a little strange for you, but you will come to love him as I already do." Katna smiled at Concha and started to wipe off the blood-spattered new born.

Concha kept crying for three days. She could not stop. She was letting out all the pain and sadness that had cast a cloud of gloom over her five years of life. However, now her mother was being so nice to her. She felt that something was wrong. The young child could not understand all that she was feeling. She could understand that a new person was coming into her life. In time, she would come to know that she would not have the experience that other children in Uxmal had with their siblings. In a week, he was wondering around the town. Everyone was surprised to see him. No one ever saw a midget, no less a bald one with piercing black eyes. From the day he came out of the egg, he had a very strange personality. He also had many psychic abilities. He would walk through the town, and he would tell people what their names were. He did not need to be introduced. It was as if he had all the knowledge of his mother and even more.

Dinner For Two

"We are at Uxmal, mi Corazon," Enrique stated from the front seat of the Mercedes. Concha heard Enrique's voice, and it brought her out of the dream state. Even though she was awake, she was still tired. Nevertheless, she knew that she had to get up. Concha knew it was imperative that she see her brother. She realized that the car was sitting in the parking lot of the Uxmal ruins. "Lift me up. I am very tired." Enrique did as he was told. He was in love with Concha. So was his friend who came to live with them, Eduardo. Enrique liked having the tall, slender Eduardo as part of their love triangle. Enrique was short and muscular. He liked making love to Eduardo too. However, his heart belonged to Concha and she knew it.

"What is the matter with you, mi Amor? You are acting like an old lady!" Eduardo had never seen her like this, nor had Enrique. Concha only laughed as Eduardo stood by the back seat where Concha's head was and lifted her up to a sitting position. He went to the other side of the car and pulled on her legs until her feet were resting on the pavement of the parking lot. She was successful at standing up. When she felt steady on her feet, she straightened out her tour guide outfit.

"I'll be back to myself soon. Then I will play with the boys with a zeal that will shock even them." Concha was trying to focus on the positive aspects of what she was about to do. Concha took a few deep

46

breaths. Her thick, wavy black hair was not happy with the tour guide hair do. She was ready, if not up for, the task at hand: find a woman to be Ixma's dinner.

She looked at a group of people who were just getting off the tour bus. They had arrived just in time to see the evening light show at the Governor's Palace. It was an ornate, rectangular building next to the Pyramid of the Magician. As the night started to become dark, there was an announcement in Spanish and English that the presentation at the Governor's Palace would now begin. Concha knew this was her cue to approach the two teenage girls that had just gotten off the bus.

Concha hurriedly walked about 20 feet out in front of them, and then let it seem that they were discovering her as they moved forward. They actually bumped into her. "Perfect" Concha thought, as she turned to face them and flashed her immaculate smile.

"Hello, ladies," she said sweetly. The girls giggled as they expressed their joy at being called ladies. "I am an official tour guide, Concha Gonzalez, at your service." She showed them her badge that reflected the validity of the statement she had just uttered.

"Would you like to see the light show from the top of the large pyramid?" The girls looked at each other, nodded an enthusiastic YES as they smiled eagerly.

"Follow me. I know a secret entrance." One could not use the stairs on the outside of the pyramid to get to the top anymore. The stairs had been chained off due to the crumbling of the stones from overuse. The girls did not hesitate for a moment. They were eager to follow her. Concha laughed to herself and pointed to the rear of the large pyramid. The trio started to walk toward the rear of the pyramid.

Concha was very careful where she was walking. She had a flashlight that she used to illumine the way for the girls. There was a lot of rubble from excavation of the site. Concha started to feel anxious; she knew that she needed to get the girls through this area without mishap. She did not want them to feel that it was too difficult and lose interest.

As the ingénues walked under the pointed, Mayan arch into the interior of the pyramid, Concha recognized that her work was almost done. She led the way into the interior of the pyramid. In a short time they arrived at a side tunnel. Concha had made sure years ago that the tunnel was clear of rubble. It needed to appear like it was a traveled corridor. Not long after the schoolgirls entered the small passageway, the trio passed by the marker that Concha was seeking: an open metal doorway. As she got close to the door Concha knew it was time to enact a carefully rehearsed set of moves. She was now leading them to their destiny. In an instant, Concha mustered all her strength. She swiftly darted behind the girls, pushed them through the doorway and slammed the ancient metal door shut. Then she secured it behind them. The door could not be opened from the inside without special knowledge of its workings.

Concha leaned against the door, exhausted. She heard the girls screaming her name, pounding on the door. Concha had to walk down the main passageway. The screams made her feel guilty, yet Concha knew that if the girls didn't die, she would. Concha walked about 100 feet down the main tunnel when the incredible, ear shattering screams erupted from within the sealed chamber.

Concha waited almost a half-hour after the shrieks had ceased to knock on the door. She had learned the hard way, with a scar on her fingers to show for it, that she did not want to disturb her brother before he was ready to see her. She knocked to let him know that she was there. She needed him now.

Slowly, the door opened. It was dark inside yet Concha entered in quickly. She knew what was there. She had entered into Ixma's lair many times in the past centuries.

"Brother," she called softly and held out her hand. She felt his small, cold, fingers grasp hers. She fell to her knees in front of him, opened her mouth and put her head back. Ixma brought his lips close to hers. Then he opened his mouth, and a vapor- like smoke came from his lips. She closed her eyes and let out a sound of relief as she felt the life force of the young girls flow into her body. She was being permeated with the quintessence of the teen-age girls. Their bodies were shriveled and tossed to the back of the room.

The room had a foot-high platform that served as a bed for the conjuror. Yes, he was the dancer. He was the magician. He was also a midget. That was his real body. The handsome, well hung performer was an image that Ixma could project into the minds of others. Then they would see him as an attractive, virile man. It took expertise to do that. The Atole was laden with herbs that made the fire ceremony attendees receptive to his mental projections. Herbs were placed into all the participants' drinks. Only the intended victim got the heavy dose.

Concha knew they were lucky tonight. Two at one time was very good. Concha could feel the stolen energy renewing her body. "If I do not have Ixma's gift every three months, I would look just like those bodies in the corner," she thought thankfully. She needed to do her part to keep this arrangement going. She and her brother were facing a crisis.

"Last night was disastrous, sister. I was weak from not feeding. The blinding, green flash of light that came out of the woman's heart sent me to the near-by ruins of Kabah. By the time I got back here, I was exhausted. When I got back to my chamber, I lay down and covered myself with the protective blanket. Shortly after I lay down and closed my eyes, I was visited by a she-demon. At first, I just heard her laugh. It was a wicked, mocking laugh. When I opened my eyes, I saw her floating around the room. She was wearing long, black tattered robes that moved as if she was floating in water. Her eyes were ablaze with green light. I sensed that she wanted to attack me, but could not get through the barrier created by the protective symbols of the Ancestors. She cackled and flew around the room and then left."

"This is not good brother. Will you ask mother if she can guide us in this matter?" the bewildered and terrified Concha pleaded.

"I will do that now. Be seated. I will call to her." Concha sat down on the floor of the cell and rested her back against the platform. Concha stared straight ahead, waiting for the blue smoke to appear. That signaled that their mother was with them. When she saw the aqua vapor, Concha sighed deeply and closed her eyes. She could not perceive her mother's words. That was only for Ixma. Many minutes passed as Concha heard her brother mumbling. He was conversing with the mist that embodied their mother's spirit. When the cloud disappeared, Concha knew that the communion was over.

"You have to find out where she is from," Ixma stated emphatically. " Mama says that she must be from across the great water that brought us the return of KuKhulKan. We have no knowledge of that land and its people. Our mother also says that we can destroy her through the old Mayan game of handball. She must be beheaded according to the ancient laws of the sacred sport. If I overpower her unfairly, mama and I fear that the she-demon will return to seek vengeance on me. Go sister, and find out where she is. Prepare her for the competition. Get that lazy

51

shaman you employ to teach her how to play the game. Those two lovers of yours know how to move in the Underworld. You have had your way with them enough times in the Underworld. They can watch her and see how she is doing."

"We must enact the sport according to our traditions. The Lords of Night will be in attendance and will enjoy the contest. She cannot slay me. She does not know how. Nor do you, my dear sister." He smiled at Concha. "You have a great deal of work to do. Now go. I do not want to waste any more energy. I have already used too much life force to talk to mother. I must now rest until the Spring Equinox. I need to sleep and dream of the game. I will use her body to pleasure myself and then take her Itza, the dew of life."

Ixma was beginning to get aroused just thinking of Morgan's statuesque form. He started to imagine her smell. He smiled, chortled and sauntered to the other side of the cell. He always had sexual interaction with his victims before he sucked them dry.

Concha heard a moan, and she knew that her brother was relieving himself of the passion that the green eyed beauty stirred within him. In a few moments, a happier looking Ixma came to the place where Concha rested.

"Go my sister, and find out what power lies within her tradition." The decaying midget lay down on his slab and used a special black cloth to cover himself. It had designs embroidered upon it. The cloth was covered with Mayan glyphs of protection and eternal life, in colors of the four directions. Red was for fire and the path of the East. Black represented the way of the West and water. Yellow stood for the earth and the South. White symbolized the North and the home of the Ancestors.

Concha closed the inner door to the chamber and pushed the outer door open, as it had been when she came there. Concha was left with the task of removing the dead bodies of the two girls. They were very light. It was not hard for Concha to drag them up the narrow, inside stairs that led to the top of the pyramid. "It is strange that these steps, that the priests used to magically appear before the festival crowds, are now used to keep us alive. We are here long after the priests!" Concha laughed to herself as she dragged the bodies up the stairs. She took a moment to enjoy the view, which the young girls never got to see, at the top of the pyramid. She threw the bodies to the jungle animals that would soon have an unexpected dinner.

Concha let out a big shout of joy when she approached the car and her waiting lovers. She opened the back door, gestured to Enrique and made it clear that she wanted him with her in the back seat. Eduardo drove them home with a big smile on his face. Laughter and shrieks of delightful surprise came from the rear seat all the way back to Playa Del Carmen.

The Blue Eyed Shaman

Morgan awoke to the sound of someone standing over her, yelling her name. She was lying face down in wet sand. She thought to herself, "I must be alive. I can feel the cold of the ocean." She was glad that someone was calling her name. Morgan hoped that she was about to be rescued. She used her arms to push herself up and sit back on her haunches. Her hands dug into the wet sand. She could feel the presence of a man repeating her name with the rich, soothing tones of his voice. Yet she kept her eyes closed. She needed a moment to get her balance and to brace herself for what she might see when she opened them.

She was quietly overjoyed to see a fine-looking man kneeling across from her on the sunlit beach. Morgan's automatic, male appraisal meter started to work. The first impression: curly, shoulder length, salt and pepper hair. Sapphire blue eyes, a tanned, lean body and a cunningly inviting smile. "A mature, very attractive, Latino gentleman," was her evaluation of the man who had come to rescue her.

She gave him a quick smile and tried to stand up. That was not so easy, and she needed help from this attractive stranger. "Did the lawyers send you to get me?" Morgan asked as she accepted his hand for support. In an instant, they both got to a standing position.

Her question evoked a tremendous belly laugh from the appealing stranger. "No, they did not send me. An incredibly sexy woman with long, curly black hair and eyes of green fire came to me in a dream. Her hair was moving as if she was floating in water. She told me that I was her kin. Then she showed me a map of what I knew was Cozumel. There was a bright green light blinking on the map. She said I had to go to this spot and find you. She then showed me a picture of you. You look just like the image she gave me, except all wet." He laughed quietly at his personal joke as he helped her to stay steady on her feet.

"Who was that woman?" Morgan asked the stranger. Even though Morgan didn't know why, she seemed to be fixated on the female with the moving black hair. "It wasn't my mother or grandmother. My mother is a red head, and grandma could never be called sexy."

"Actually, she looked a lot like Elvira, the Halloween lady," the new arrival into Morgan's life stated politely.

"Oh boy," Morgan thought to herself as she started to assess the situation and walk around in circles. "Here I am on an island in the middle of who- knows- where, with an attractive, but albeit, strange man. " OK." Morgan said, as she faced her rescuer. "Some sexed- out chick with electric hair came to you in a dream and told you where to find me. Please know that I am very thankful you are here. I have no idea who the woman could be. If you could bring me back to the language school, I would greatly appreciate it." She made an effort to sound authoritative, but the charming man only laughed. And laughed and laughed. It took him a few moments to compose himself.

"Please excuse me for laughing at your plight," he said politely. "You cannot go back to the language school. You cannot go anywhere right now. You have to stay here until Concha, my boss, sends me to find you. She doesn't know that I have made contact with you. I am sure that she will send many people to look for you. I sense that I am supposed to be of assistance to you. I'm not sure what that entails just yet, but what is really important is that you are safe. I am pledged to assist you."

"Pledged to assist me? " Morgan repeated.

"Yes. I gave the woman with the fiery green eyes my word. I told her that I would find you and help you in any way I can. I drank from a chalice that she gave me in the dream. The contents of the cup were very sweet. My impression is that the drink sealed the bargain between us. I felt very good after it all." The man replied. "I don't want to get on the wrong side of your friend, the Elvira lady. "

"She is not my friend. I have no idea who she is!" Morgan was very confused, and her famous Irish temper was getting ready to flare up. "What has happened to me? "Before the man had a chance to answer, Morgan yelled in a demanding tone "Where am I?"

"You are on the island of Cozumel. How you got here; I don't know. There was a huge sound like a sonic boom and flash in the sky last night. It was an enormous green light. Why you are here is very complicated. I want to tell you the whole story when I have time to give you all the details. I will return tomorrow. When I come back, we will take a ferry to the mainland, and then I will be able to enlighten you about the entire situation. Now is not the time. You must rest now. I have brought you some water, food and a blanket that will sustain you until I can come back for you."

"I feel he is a kind man. I sense that I can trust him," Morgan thought to herself.

"We have to move you to a hiding place. You are too exposed out here. I know of an area that has trees that will protect you until I come back. "He approached her and put a hat on her head that had a big, floppy brim. "After you." He extended his arm in the direction of the shore line and a small grove of trees. He carried the large tote bag filled with food and water.

In about ten minutes, they arrived at the spot that had some foliage and a little sandy beach area "You will be safe here until I return." He smiled as they approached a cluster of trees that went right to the edge of the ocean. After she had situated herself among the trees, he handed her the bag of food and turned to go. "Stay out of the sun and away from passersby. Do not leave this area. I know it is lonely, but your safety depends on it. "

Morgan smiled at her savior. "Thanks for all the help."

"I am not sure what is coming for you. However, I know that it will be unlike anything you are able to imagine. Don't allow your thoughts to dwell on anything fearful. That will only hurt you. Keep your mind on something that makes you feel love and happiness. Know and believe that you are safe." He smiled and Morgan felt some comfort within her. The warmth made her feel that he was speaking the truth. "Don't worry. I will explain all to you at the right time. Now it is imperative that you rest. I will be back for you soon," he smiled.

"This guy has a great smile. I feel he is a loving, caring man." Morgan thought to herself.

"Open the bag," he politely requested. He pointed to the large tote bag of food he had set down on the sand. Morgan did as he suggested and found a feast of tortillas, chicken, avocados and rice inside. There were also six large bottles of drinking water and a grey and white striped blanket. The gentleman watched her as she carefully examined the contents of the bag. She dug out a bottle of water and the fluid quickly disappeared. The man grinned at Morgan and then turned to leave.

"What is your name?" Morgan asked as he started to walk away. "You seem to know mine"

"My name is Felipe. I am shaman and healer in Playa Del Carmen." He thought for a moment and then added. "If you can believe just one thing, know that I am here to help you. I do not want to aggravate that woman who came to me in the dream. I know that she is real. I don't know who she is: a spirit, a ghost, maybe a dead relative. One thing is for sure. She has great power, and I want her to be pleased. Keeping you safe is keeping her happy."

"Thank you," Morgan replied. As he was walking away, Morgan called out to him. "I do trust you. A lot of things have happened. I do not know what to think."

"The important thing is not to worry. Even though you don't know what is going on, I sense that you will emerge from this situation a better, stronger woman." With that he waved good-by and walked off. Morgan kept staring at him until he was out of sight. She desperately wanted clarity about her situation. Even so, Morgan knew what she need to do, what she hated to do: be patient.

Even though Morgan desired to know why she was sitting on a deserted beach waiting for a charming man to return, the grumbling in her stomach told her that she needed to eat. She looked at the bag and started to rummage through its contents. In a few moments, she was chomping down on a tasty chicken taco. "Wow this is good!" she thought as she quickly ingested the meal. Then she started on the bottles of water. "Well, I am getting back in touch with my body. Now it's telling me that I am really tired." The feeling of fullness in her digestive system was beckoning her to sleep. She looked for a flat area that was covered completely from the sun. Her clothes had dried during the walk on the beach. She was not cold, and was enjoying the mild afternoon sun of winter. After smoothing out the sand, she lay down and covered herself with the blanket. It only took a few minutes for Morgan to be engulfed in a deep sleep.

She had been slumbering for a few hours when she received a visit from her grandmother in the dream state. Morgan suddenly saw herself back at the Malibu estate that she loved so much. In the dream she was taking her horse, Raven, for a slow walk to the beach. She was not sitting on Raven, but she was walking beside him, holding the reigns loosely. It was a bright Malibu morning and Morgan could even feel the gentle sun on her arms and head. She was wearing a long flowing gown of green. Her hair was loose and moving a bit in the soft breeze. As Morgan and Raven were strolling to the beach, her grandmother suddenly appeared on the path, blocking their progress. She looked different then Morgan had known her to be. Her hair was still long and white as Morgan remembered, but her eyes were a bright green. In real life, her eyes had been blue. Her wrinkles were gone, and her skin looked youthful and radiant. She did not look tired and downhearted as she had before her death.

"Your awakening has begun Morgan," she said as she put her hand on Raven's nose. "It is time for you to start your mission on earth. I have not been able to contact you before now. That has been the wish of the great goddess that we serve, The Morrighan. It is our duty to be of assistance to her. The women in our family have been pledged to do her bidding throughout all eternity. Your mother and I were together as priestesses in another life. That is why we came together in this life. Now it is your turn. She will let you know what she wants you to do when the time is right. Now you have to trust the route that has brought you to her service. You are doing exactly what you were born to do. Your mother had a vision of your future when you were just five. She saw that you were going to take up arms for The Morrighan. I have passed on to you the great knowledge of our house. Remember our lessons, for they will provide you with all that you need to succeed. Your mother helped me place the Shield of Protection in your heart. We both knew that was all we could do to keep you from harm. Now the defense is gone. We cannot replace it. You have the ancestry of our most valiant champions within you. It is time for your abilities to emerge.

You must embrace your new mission. For now, all that is important for you to know is that you are not alone. Please go with that nice man who found you. He is your guardian for the time being. He will keep you from harm. You can trust him. Don't fight the adventure. You can be so headstrong at times. Have faith and know that the Holy Virgin is also with you. You have not met her yet, but she will help you. I love you more than anyone can ever measure. Your mother does as well. She had to disconnect from you when you married. Have faith in the process that you are going through. You are now coming face to face with your destiny. I know you will probably remember little of this when you awaken. Rest now my beloved and know that all is as it needs to be." With that grandma Molly faded away. Then Morgan mounted Raven and rode off along the path.

Revelations

Morgan slept until the next day. She awoke just before dawn. When she was fully conscious and had eaten a bit of breakfast, she got up. Walking was a bit tough. Her legs were stiff from lack of use. "Think I will do some yoga. That will help me stretch out my unhappy legs." She had never had such stiff muscles. After about a half-hour of poses, she thought "I am getting my body back." She could walk much better after the yoga. She did not feel it would be a wise idea to take a stroll along the beach, even though her body was begging her to do just that. Her intuition, that seemed to be working a bit, told her that she needed to stay put. Felipe could come back at any time. Nevertheless, she needed to do something.

"I am thankful that I had a lot of lessons. I think I will just do QiGong for a bit. That will give my body a stretch and will ground and center me more. I can see now it was a blessing that I had the opportunity to learn so many disciplines that are coming in handy." She stayed under the cover of the trees and became lost in the smooth, flowing moves of the Chinese exercises. "I feel that my head is finally getting clear. I have felt so fogged over since the divorce started. This is really refreshing!" She was beginning to feel energy circulating through her system again. The sensation was usually second nature to her. The experience had disappeared when the divorce started. "Thank you, powers-that-be for helping me!" Then she sat down, had another snack and started her meditation practice.

"At least the time I spent with Gerard gave me the opportunity to learn so much that seems to be helping me now," she thought pensively. Then another wave of thankfulness washed over her. She realized that she had been given a lot of opportunities to improve herself physically, mentally and spiritually.

Now, thinking about Gerard and what she had been forced to give up just made her sad. She started to cry, but she found that she did not go through one of her the major crying fits that had been part of her life for the last three months. She did have to go through her ritual. She took out Gerard's picture from her bag and looked at it again. She still felt melancholy when she looked at him, but somehow losing him did not seem so painful now.

"Maybe I am getting over the divorce. I do feel better emotionally then I have in months. I am finally starting to feel that I can move on and leave Gerard behind," she thought and looked out over the rhythmic sea. "Maybe it is the ocean. The sea air feels like it is revitalizing my body when I breathe it in." She took in a deep breath and felt invigorated. "I did feel the best when I was with Gerard at the Malibu house. I am getting the impression that the ocean water is activating something within me." Morgan sat up straight with crossed legs, taking in as much of the moist, salty air as her lungs could hold. She kept feeling better and better with each breath. "Strange as this may be for my current state of affairs, I feel really great!" After a few minutes of staring at the ocean and breathing in deeply, Morgan felt liveliness permeating all her cells and recharging her system.

Morgan decided to adopt a new attitude. "Í am just going to do what grandma said to do in my dream," Morgan told herself. "I am going to trust that all will be ok. Then she laughed out loud. "I don't care what is making me feel this way; I am just thankful and happy that I finally feel ok. I am so glad to feel whole, not splintered apart." Then, for some reason, not known to her conscious mind, Morgan felt moved to kneel and give thanks for her rescue and safety.

"Thank you Ocean, Grandma and whoever has helped me to be here. I want to thank all the invisible powers that have saved me and brought me to this safe place. I don't know who you are, lady with the big black hair, but you are helping me, and I want to give you a big Thank You." With that, Morgan held her hands up to her face and blew a kiss into them. Then she opened her arms and turned her hands toward the sea, as if to share the kiss with the ocean.

After basking in the glow of gratitude for a few moments, she got back to her meditation. She had learned a mantra and the way to use it from the Transcendental Meditation organization. The group had a center right near her familial home in Santa Monica. She had learned before she met Gerard. Grandma had insisted that she needed to learn contemplation. She started to sink deep into the altered states of meditation. While she was meditating, with her legs crossed and her spine erect, she heard a voice call her name in a strong, but muted whisper.

"Morgan. It is Felipe. I have returned. We can go back to the mainland. I will explain everything on the trip." She opened her jade colored eyes. Morgan looked at him with an expression that was deeply serene.

Your aura is much calmer today. It appears as if the rhythms of the waves and the sea air have acted like a healing balm for your emotions. Your energy field is calm and peaceful this morning. Maybe Ix Chel has brought you some healing."

"It could be." Morgan said, starting to giggle like a little girl. "I have had a great time here with the ocean. I feel soothed yet energized."

"This is the island dedicated to IX Chel, the Mayan goddess of the moon, the tides and childbirth. She may be talking to you. I feel that she helped to bring you here. I also sense that at some point, it would be wise of you to return to give thanks and an offering to her"

"Wow, I was just thinking how thankful I am to be here!"

"She may be speaking to you already. I have a relative who is very devoted to IX Chel. This Mayan goddess is still very much alive in the hearts of many of us."

"Oookkkkk" Morgan said with a shred of skepticism in the tone of her voice. "I am game for anything that will help."

Felipe gave her a sideways look. He brought her some flip flops for the journey. He set them down in front of her. "You are not a believer in the power of the Goddess?"

"I have to be honest," Morgan thought to herself. She felt that she could not afford to be dishonest. She believed that many invisible eyes, Grandma's in particular, were watching her. "I am not sure," she said to Felipe. "I am not opposed to it, but I just don't know much about goddesses. I guess I would need some tangible experience with a goddess to really make me a believer. There were a lot of my friends, who are not my friends anymore, who liked to dress up and play at being goddesses. They used to have ceremonies and full moon gatherings. I never felt any substantial power at the get-togethers. They were nothing like the ceremonies that my mother and grandmother did. It was easy to feel the power that they generated.

"Is it the goddess or your former friends whom you are angry with?"

That last statement caused Morgan to lower her head. "Well, I have no reason to be upset with the goddess. It is the women I thought were my friends," she said as she looked up into Felipe's face. The sadness of her reality in Los Angeles began to return to her. He could hear the despair in her voice as she continued. "They all deserted me when they heard that Gerard and I were getting a divorce. I see now that in those social circles, a wife is just supposed to keep quiet and not make a fuss about anything. I guess my feisty Irish temper motivated me to find out where and with whom he was sharing his affection." Morgan concluded, reacting to the old feelings of betrayal.

"Oh, so you are Irish. Concha will be happy to know that. She has been told by her brother to discover the source of your magic. I will tell her that you are Irish. Then they will understand where the enchantment came from that protected you. Gather up the stuff. Put your hat on. I will explain more on the ferry. It is time for you to go back to the mainland." He turned away from her and started to walk down the beach.

His action plunged Morgan into a state of panic. "Hold on, wait a second. Let me get the bag…" She grabbed her purse and the bag that Felipe had given her. She quickly put on the flip-flops and hurried after him. "I have to follow him. He is my life line to the world." Morgan thought to herself and added mentally "Not just the world, but a hot shower and hopefully a salad!" she giggled to herself. Morgan was soon able to come up beside him and match his stride.

"You are a fast walker" she said, trying to make some conversation. "I hope you are just as fast of a talker. As in telling me how I can get back in touch with the lawyers. They will straighten this all out"

Much to her surprise, Felipe started laughing hysterically as he walked. He laughed so hard that he had to hold his stomach. "Oh dios mio, you are entertaining."

"Ok. What is the big joke?" Morgan demanded to know. The hair on the back of her neck was beginning to rise. "I didn't think what I said was that funny"

"Oh but it was, my dear. Please forgive me for laughing at your expense. It is the lawyers who put you here in the first place." After he said that he turned back in the direction they were going and acted as if he wanted to ignore her .He knew that this was the beginning of Morgan's understanding of her present situation. He knew he had to be patient with her.

"What do you mean???" There was more than a little twinge of tension in her voice. "You need to explain NOW, SENOR!" she said in a loud, perturbed voice.

"Ok,Ok,Ok, Well, how do I put this? "

"Just spit it out! No frills, no sugar coating. I want the truth!!! " She yelled.

Felipe stopped walking and thought for a moment. He realized that it might be better to give her the news in bits that she can digest a little at a time. He turned to her and let the first bomb drop. "At your husband's request, the lawyers made arrangements for you to be killed." Felipe turned away and continued to walk toward the port where they would catch the ferry. He said nothing more. He knew that it would not be easy for her to ingest all that he had to share with her.

"Wwwwhaaaat?" Was all that she could say.

"It was your lawyers, at your husband's request, who arranged this trip for you. You were supposed to kiss the Mayan dancer and die." They walked in silence as the pair left the beach area and came into civilization. Felipe turned around a few times to make sure she was following him. He could feel the intensity of her emotions. His work as a shaman made it easy for him to feel her agitated mental body. She was trying desperately to fit the new information into the framework of what she felt was her reality. They were approaching the ferry dock and crowds of waiting people.

Morgan had settled into a state of deep emotional distress. The turmoil in her mind kept her silent. She was not ready to hear the details. She felt conflicted, thinking about the lawyers. They had been so kind and nurturing to her through the whole divorce ordeal. "The lawyers arranged for my death. How could that be?" Morgan's traumatized mind was in the middle of going back over all the events of the last three months as they started to board the ferry. It would take her to the mainland and to a new and uncertain situation.

"Keep your hat on and your head down. Here, put on these sunglasses. Your picture has been in all the papers and on TV." Felipe handed her the sunglasses he had been wearing. This last morsel of information caused Morgan's new-found shock to grow. Felipe handled the transactions for the trip back to the mainland of Mexico. Morgan followed him quietly, and as instructed, had her head down and gave the impression that she was a humble woman following her man on board. In truth, Morgan had gone completely numb. Felipe walked to the back of the ferry, sat down on the benches that bordered the boat and leaned back against the railing. He patted the seat next to him with his hand and Morgan collapsed into it. The truth had become an oppressive weight. She was still not prepared to converse. It took all her strength just to lean back against the rail, close her eyes and tilt her head back to let the sun caress her face. She was overwhelmed by all that she had found out in the last half hour. Morgan turned away from him, lost in the chaos that was exploding in her psyche. Felipe looked at her closely and then turned away.

"She is not ready to talk." That was his instant appraisal of Morgan's new mental status. "She is not prepared to learn more at the moment." Felipe thought, as he let his intuition speak to him. It was a 40-minute back to the mainland, so he felt that at some point in the journey, she would be ready for more. "I don't know what my part in this play is yet. I do feel that I am meant to help her. Of this, I am sure. Maybe the sexy mama that came to me in my dream will return and tell me what I am supposed to do. I wouldn't mind seeing her again, preferably in a bikini!" He had to laugh out loud at his thoughts. He was a man, a single man. He has no woman in his life at the moment. "I don't want to piss off the dream wench. She could make my life miserable," he chuckled to himself. He was not a fool. He knew that any being that could carry on a conversation with him in the dream must have substantial capabilities. He reflected on the pact that he made with the goddess. Then he turned to face the woman in his charge. A thought came to him that she was like the wind. She had come to blow away the evil that had been hovering over him and so many others.

As the ferry headed toward the mainland of Playa Del Carmen, Felipe stayed quiet. "She will let me know when she wants to hear more," he told himself. He was content to be in the wind, enjoying the cool air that came off the ocean at this time of the year. His thoughts drifted to the approaching holiday. "Christmas is only a couple of days away. I need to get some presents for Lupe and her family." They were his only family these days. He, better than most people, understood what Morgan was going through."She is experiencing the Shaman's Death. My Shaman's Death was not so dramatic. I lost my birth family and the life I had with them. Morgan has lost everything. She has no one but me to help her. This means that she is going through a very powerful transformation. She is a woman of power, of that I am sure. Now is the time for her to become acquainted with her abilities. She will need them all for what she must face when we get off this ferry."

As his thoughts glided back to Morgan, he turned to face her. Her face was still turned away from him, apparently lost in thought. His instinctual male side started to take pleasure in her loveliness. He looked at her a long while, without her knowing. He thought her hair was incredible. Even though it was matted and full of sand, he could see that her long tresses were exquisite. Her hair was the color of the midnight sky. Her eyes were a dark shade of green like the sacred wells, the Cenotes. Her slim nose, high cheekbones and full lips were inviting even when they did not wish to be. Felipe had never seen such a delicate, slender neck on a woman in the Yucatan. It was clear that her genetic roots were somewhere in Europe.

As she shifted her body toward him, he felt he should look away. He did not want her to feel that he was staring at her small breasts. She did not have a bra on. When he found her, he could see the outline of her nipples as her wet blouse clung to them. Now her blouse was dry, and it hid their allure. It was obvious that she exercised a great deal, because her abdomen was firm. There was nothing extra on her hips, for the shape of her torso made that clear. But her legs. They excited him the most. He enjoyed looking at the strong, well defined muscles. Even her feet were superb. They were long and slender. She still had red polish on her toes that he found enticing. He loved feet!

Suddenly, she stood up. She put her hands on her hips and bent her torso from side to side. She did several stretches before she sat down, turned to Felipe and said. "OK I am ready to hear it. Let her rip!"

"Let her rip?" he came back with a question. He did not understand that idiom. His English was learned during his early years in school. Then it was strengthened by his contact with many Americans through his healing practice. Even so, he was not able to stay abreast of all the American slang.

"Yes. That means tell we what is going on with my life, please!" She sat down on the bench quickly. The tone in her voice was not as hostile, it was pleading.

"Si, Senora" he said quietly.

"You mean Senorita. I am single now, very single," she said with a twinge of grief in her voice.

"At your service, Senorita" He said. He sat up, cleared his throat and then started to talk. "You are a victim. You are a victim of a plot to kill you that was orchestrated by your lawyers and your husband." He stopped after that statement to see how she was doing.

"Go on" she said.

"She did not flinch or react when I said that," he thought to himself. "She must be a warrior, even if she doesn't know it. She composed herself in a short amount of time. She may succeed after all," he reflected.

74

"The sexy Mayan dancer," Felipe started, "was Ixma, a magician from the ancient Mayan city of Uxmal. The ruins of the city are a couple of hours away from here. He is really a midget who is over 3,000 years old. The extremely attractive serving woman, Concha, who gave you the Atole at the fire ceremony, is also that old. You noticed that Concha is gorgeous and healthy? That is because her brother keeps her and himself alive by sucking the life force out of innocent women. He takes the energy that is generated by breathing in and out. That is what keeps the body alive. Without that, the body dies."

"By Life Force, do you mean something like Chi or Prana? Morgan asked, referring back to the knowledge that Shuru, the Yoga teacher, shared with her.

"Yes. That is it exactly. He can connect with that force within each person and extract it. The ancient Mayan term for the life force is Itz. " Felipe commented. After a moment, he continued. "He takes the life force of women who rich men want to see disappear. There have been many mistresses that have been sent to the language school to be taught a deadly lesson. Ixma doesn't feed off people that might be missed."

That last statement hit a nerve with Morgan. She knew that there was no one who would try to find out what happened to her. Felipe saw Morgan react to these words physically. She clinched her teeth, sat up straight and started rubbing her thighs. Her head was bent down. There was silence. Felipe was waiting for a sign from Morgan that would let him know she was ready to hear more.

Morgan felt tears coming into her eyes. She allowed them to roll down her cheeks before she wiped them away. "Ok." After a few moments and a lot of swallows, she picked her head up and stared toward the front of the boat. She let her hands come to rest on her knees to brace herself for whatever may come next.

"Ixma, the dancer, shares the life force with Concha so that she can keep a steady flow of women coming to Boca Negra. She is Ixma's contact in our world. With the media as it is these days, they cannot keep using random people without searches taking place. The police can only be bribed so much.

As you might have already guessed, the drink that Concha gave you that night was loaded with a powerful hallucinogen that has been used by the Maya since olden times. The drug causes you to feel no physical pain. It makes you feel blissful. It can also give you visions. The sacrificial victims whom the Maya offered to the Lords of the Night did not object or react in fear as the Obsidian blade came toward them. All of Mayan society used the drug for ceremonial bloodletting and to observe handball games in the Underworld. The kings and queens used to take the drug when they had to perform public ceremonial bloodletting. The legend goes that the Ancestors, the Mayan elders who are said to watch over us from the Underworld, also observe the sacrifices and the handball games. The living Maya have to observe the rules of the Lords of Night and the Ancestors when in the Underworld or suffer horrific consequences. The Lords of Night can be cruel, but they have also been known to be merciful. It is said that the Lords of Night love to see a good fight. They derive great amusement from seeing the struggles of humans that reside in the upper world. That is why the handball game was invented. They have been lenient to those that played the game valiantly."

"Wow," was the only comment that Morgan made.

"You took a large dose of that same drug. That is why you could enter the Mayan Underworld. That is also the reason that the people that you saw at Uxmal could not see you. You were in the Mayan Underworld."

"What is the Underworld?" Morgan questioned. She desired more information about this extraordinary place.

"It is the dwelling place of the Lords of Night and the Ancestors. The Lords of Night have never been mortal, but the Ancestors are departed Maya from times of old. To the Maya, there are the Lords of the Day, which govern life on the top of the earth. Then there are the Lords of Night who rule the Underworld. The Underworld is the realm of death and rebirth. It is where the souls of the Maya go to rest and then be reborn. The Eastern religions also have this concept in their beliefs.

The Underworld can be entered in several ways. It exists in another dimension or frequency but has the identical geographic location on the earth. It is still in the same time and space as the world we are in now, but it is another plane of existence, another frequency. You can enter the Underworld by taking the drug and using the dark portals, such as the one at Boca Negra. During the Solstices and Equinoxes the portals can be used to go to the Underworld without the drug. The Underworld can also be entered through certain caves. Mayan shamans know which caves can take you to the Underworld."

"Ok." Morgan said, "This a bit much for me to wrap my head around. Yet, I have to admit that what you have said about the Mayan Underworld is exactly what I experienced with the Mayan performer the other night," she stated. Her intuition, that now seemed to be in high gear, was also telling her that he was speaking the truth.

"Wrap your head around?" Felipe said.

"To digest mentally" she explained.

"Well, don't worry about that. You will have plenty of opportunities to experience the Mayan Underworld. You will be taking the drug many times. You will learn how to maneuver in the Underworld.

"Is this going to be like the mushroom trips I took in high school?" Morgan asked.

"You must realize that the drug is not to be used for recreation, the way that so many Americans do. It is a sacred plant. It is a teacher plant. It opens up your consciousness to experience the divine. It is also used to go to the Underworld. When you use it now, it will take you to the Underworld through the dark portals. Then you will learn to maneuver in the Underworld and play the handball game so that you can destroy Ixma"

"Could you repeat that again? DESTROY IXMA??? What is this about DESTROY? Should I take that to mean that I must KILL SOMEONE???" The tension in Morgan's voice had grown by many decimals.

Felipe did not react to her remarks. He knew that she had to let her emotions out. He sensed that this was necessary in order to prepare her for the challenge ahead. "You must. Or he will kill you. He needs you dead to keep his business and the life force flowing. He wants to defeat you in a way that will not invoke any retaliation from the Elvira lady. She also paid a call on Ixma. She could not get past his protection, but he realizes that she could get him any time he leaves his den. Ixma is terrified of her. He calls her a she-demon. He is afraid that if he kills you unfairly, he will leave himself open for vengeance from her. That is why he will contest you according to the traditions of his magic. He believes that if he vanquishes you according to the ancient rules of the Mayan handball game, he will be protected by the Lords of Night and the Ancestors from retaliation. He wants to kill you in front of the Lords of Night and the Ancestors." Felipe paused for a moment and next added, "He is not the attractive man whom you saw dancing at Boca Negra and on top of the pyramid at Uxmal. "

"How did you know about that" Morgan said in an astonished tone. She was shocked that he knew what had happened. She didn't notice anyone else there except the hunky dancer. Morgan began to blush. "Did he see me doing all my sex gyrations?" Morgan wondered to herself, feeling embarrassed.

"How cute, she is blushing!" Felipe thought. He suddenly realized that Morgan had been motivated to express herself sexually when she was with Ixma on the Pyramid of the Magician. Felipe was a gentleman above all else, and did not share his inner thoughts with Morgan. "I know because that is what has happened to hundreds of women. Concha, my boss, has told me what takes place with the women who drink the potion. You are not the first one. He was prevented from kissing you. You could not resist him. No woman has ever been able to resist him. The drug makes sure of that. You were saved because he was not able to touch his lips to yours. If he had been capable of doing that, you would have been locked into a sound activated force field. You would not be able to free yourself. He would have sucked the life essence out of your body." Felipe said in a serious tone. "That makes the body shrivel up like a prune. Then he brings the body back through the dark portal. That is why the little area you went to for the party is called Boca Negra. It means black mouth. It is one of the dark portals on the planet where he can come and go. One of the selling points of this system is that there will never be any witnesses. No one, in the time and space we are in right now, could see the murder taking place, even if it was enacted right in front of them in the Unerworld. He returns the body to Boca Negra and dumps it in the ocean near shore. The sea water plumps up the corpse. It looks like the woman drowned. The rich men pay Concha for disposing of their wives before the divorce is final. That way there are no alimony payments and nothing to deal with from the ex."

Morgan shot him a poignant look. She got up from her seat on the deck and started to walk around. She was definitely agitated. Felipe was patient again. He let her walk around as much as she needed. That was a lot of horrible information to absorb.

In a few moments, Morgan calmed down and went back to her seat next to Felipe. A moment of thoughtfulness engulfed Morgan. With a pensive tone in her voice she asked, "How was I saved? Why didn't I succumb like all the others? I was certainly ready to kiss him. What stopped the process?"

"That is the answer that Concha, Ixma, your lawyers and your husband want to know. What protected you? Concha and Ixma are looking for that answer. How did you get to the safety of the island? You traveled through the sky for over a hundred miles." Felipe said. "What saved you when countless women have died needlessly?"

Morgan now felt very humbled and a bit curious too. "I have no idea. I did not try to avoid the dancer. I was ready to kiss him."

"You are either blessed or cursed, Morgan," Felipe stated in a solemn tone. "Those women died because they had the misfortune to know men who really did not love them. When they were done with their wives and mistresses, they simply had them obliterated. The souls of those women are still trapped in the Underworld. That was meant to be your fate. Something more powerful than Ixma, from the time of ancient magic, stepped in to save you." Felipe said.

The pain he felt about these needless deaths obviously troubled him greatly. He fell silent. He was waiting for an answer. He did not want to rush her. She needed to process all of this traumatic information. She needed to organize her thoughts even though her mind was going in many simultaneous directions.

The humbleness of surviving a brush with death echoed in Morgan's voice. "The protection came from my grandmother," she stated softly. She knew no magic. Morgan wished now that she had listened to her grandma more. Morgan felt that her grandma was really her mother. Her own mother had been very distant. They lived in a tiny house in Santa Monica, California, right across the highway from the ocean, until she met Gerard.

"I had a dream about my grandmother while I was waiting for you to return. She said that the protective shield cannot be reused. My grandmother used to say that we had a pure blood line, that we were descended from the ancient Druids. That is all that I know." After she said that, she hoped that she had not revealed too much. She still did not know anything about this man. "I need to be on guard. I don't know what I am heading into" she told herself. She kept searching her memory about her time with her grandmother.

"Well, that explains some of it," Felipe said.

"I did feel a strange sensation in my heart area. A pressure first, and then I felt something surrounding me. It was like an air bag in a car going off. Something just opened up and encircled me. That is all I know." A moment of contrition engulfed Morgan. "I wanted to kiss the guy," Morgan admitted. "I wanted to feel good for a change. I have been miserable for over a year. It has taken me a while to face that my marriage is over." Morgan stated with a great deal of frustration in her voice. "My grandmother wanted to teach me a lot of magic. I didn't feel like learning when I grew to be a teenager. I followed her around like a new-born chick when I was little. Once puberty hit, I lost interest and got involved in life." A twinge of guilt edged with a touch of remorse had crept into Morgan's voice.

"That sounds about right actually." Felipe stated. "When a magical child reaches puberty, the magic usually goes into hiding." Felipe said with a grin.

"Don't feel bad about lost opportunities. You have died the Shaman's Death." Morgan gave him a quizzical look when he mentioned the Shaman's Death. Felipe decided to go on and not wait for Morgan to do any 'head wrapping'. "A person that is meant to become the shaman, midwife or healer of a Mayan tribe goes through some type of crisis and comes close to death. They may lose everything, for some reason, through divorce, financial disaster or family problems. The catastrophe itself is there to make the person disconnect from their old way of life.

"Once in a while, the tribe, like the Maya, will pick a person to go through the Shaman's Death. Often the person is not born into the traditional day signs of the shaman or healer, but exhibits the tendencies in their everyday life. In such a case, the Maya will single out the person and put them through it. The person will have to go on a mission. I think that the term Vision Quest has become popular with Americans. The person may have to go out in the jungle for a week, without food or water. When that is their test, they eat plants that they think are going to keep them alive, but the plants have a lesson for them. This is the way the plant medicine bonds with the new healer. Whatever plants they eat during their test will eventually become their plant helpers.

A plant helper is an herb or combination of herbs that the shaman will use to cure those that come to him. It is during the Shamans' Death that you find whatever you will use to be of service to others. That is what happened to my cousin, Lupe. You will meet her. She now works with plant medicine." Felipe said quietly. Whenever he talked of the shamanic world, he became very reverent. He had seen the power of the plants many times. "The plant or stone or other knowledge that comes on the Journey of the Shaman's Death will mark you in some way. The person may get an injury that is a reminder of their mission in life. I was lucky. I only got a scar on my right hand. I know of a man who went through the Shaman's Death and lost a leg. He became a healer that helps crippled people walk. He is giving others the gift of what was taken from him The bigger the price the shaman pays, the greater their power is to be of service to others. You have paid a high price already through the Shaman's Death."

Morgan was speechless. She was in awe of this man who seemed to be very down to earth, but had a great deal of wisdom within him. After a few moments, she said, "Well I certainly have died the Shaman's Death. I realize that I did come very close to physically dying. I don't know what new abilities will emerge, but already I can feel an enhanced connection to water, to the ocean. I feel lucky to be alive" Morgan was beginning to be touched by this man. He gave the impression of having a gentle heart. He appeared to be very caring. She found his tenderness and compassion very appealing. She did not realize that she was beginning to fall in love with him.

"You are not lucky Morgan. It was obvious to me that you were meant to go through this challenge. No humans set up this challenge for you. It was preordained. It was meant to be. It was not a mistake." Felipe suddenly changed the topic when he had a new thought. "What is your birthday? I want to find out your Mayan astrology sign. That may give us clues to your destiny here.

When Morgan told him her birth date, he quickly pulled out some charts from his back pack and did some speedy mental calculations. When he was done, he simply said, "Madre mia, now I understand"

"SO..." Morgan said, trying not to let her curiosity become too obvious.

"You are a 13 Obsidian Blade." Felipe said with a great deal of enthusiasm that Morgan did not share. "It is very clear to me. The astrology sign of Obsidian Blade in Mayan astrology is the sign of the warrior and the healer. This day sign can take life or give life. The Obsidian Blade, in olden times, was used to cut the heart out of the sacrificial victims or cut out tumors and disease from the body. It is one of the Mayan astrology signs that carried an obligation to the community. The number 13 is the highest number that can be given to an astrology sign. It is the most potent placement for an Obsidian Blade. People who are born into the number 13 usually experience great intensity and drama in their life. They achieve greatness in any area where they apply their focus. Crazy, extreme and dramatic occurrences usually happen to those born with the number 13. You are beginning to live up to the reputation of a 13 Obsidian Blade," Felipe concluded.

"I don't really feel like a warrior or a healer, but extreme does describe my life for the past nine years: the lifestyle of the extremely rich!" These last words brought up many feelings within Morgan. She felt relief at knowing that there was some reason for all that she had just experienced.

"You have gone through a lot of healing already," he said as he smiled. "I can see it in your aura. Much of what has been enraging you has now left your energy fields." Morgan smiled at him and shook her head in agreement." You still have issues to heal, Morgan. This is just the beginning." Felipe stated in a quiet, sober tone.

She laughed and nodded in accord. "I'm sure that I do." There was a peaceful tone in her voice that he had not heard before. Morgan sat up and stretched. She reached her arms over her head and brought her hands together. She felt the joy of muscular release as she stretched her arms as far as they would go. Then she bent over and touched her feet.

"You do Yoga?" Felipe asked.

Morgan laughed. "Yes. I had the good luck to be able to learn a lot of spiritual body disciplines. I learned Qi Gong. It is a type of Chinese movement exercise that is supposed to bring balance to body and spirit. I also studied meditation, Transcendental Meditation. It is a type of meditation that comes from India. A man named Deepak Chopra taught me. "

"You have been prepared then. All of these are very powerful and very old techniques for balancing and preparing the body for spiritual work."

This last statement brought a smile to Morgan's face. She did something right. Gerard always made her feel that her spiritual pursuits like meditation were useless. It was nice to meet someone who appreciated what she valued. She was beginning to feel better about herself. "I am starting to see that there is a reason for all that has happened," she said gently to Felipe. There was a reason that she had wanted to learn all the spiritual bodywork classes. This last though did give Morgan a sense that she was somewhat prepared for what was ahead of her.

"Morgan, we will be landing in Playa Del Carmen in a short time. I still have more to explain to you before we land." He gestured to Morgan to sit near him. "As I have said, I work for Concha. You really need to know more about her and her brother." Felipe continued, "You have to realize that you will be entering and working in the realms of magic. To succeed you must be willing to let go of all that you have known as reality in your old life. You need to be in the present and accept what comes. You will get a good education on how to move in the Mayan Underworld. The Mayan Underworld is a magical realm."

"OK." was her reply. Morgan sensed that what he was saying was important.

"Ixma was born of magic. He has also been given immortality through magic. So has Concha. She has been kept alive to do her brother's dirty work. They need each other to exist. They will do anything to keep this little money/life force factory that they have in operation. I have been told that he has a weak spot."

"When we first met, Concha told me the story of the way Ixma became immortal. Ixma was getting in trouble in the city of Uxmal, during the height of the Mayan empire. A different ruler took over in Uxmal. This new king had a great disdain for Ixma and wanted to do away with him. Ixma and his mother knew that his time in the city was short. Katna went back to the witch that had helped her birth Ixma. By that time Concha was a sultry young woman of 22."

"Both Concha and her mother went to visit the witch of Chichen Itza to see if there was some spell or way that Ixma could avoid the wrath of the new ruler. Katna felt that sending Ixma to another place would be pointless. By this time, his reputation had spread throughout the Mayan world."

"When they met with the witch of Chichen Itza, she said that she was not the person to help with such a task. Ixma was already beginning to deteriorate. The spell that created him had not worked exactly as planned. It is like baking a cake. Sometimes it falls"

"Yes, I get it. That is why I don't bake!" Morgan laughed.

"The witch of Chichen Itza told Concha's mother to go to the city of Tikal in Guatemala. There she would find a male witch named Mentun."

"It was then that the witch of Chichen Itza demanded the payment that she was promised, when she helped Concha's mother birth Ixma. Concha was told that she was now the property of the witch of Chichen Itza. When Concha heard this, she started to scream uncontrollably."

"The witch asked if Concha was a virgin. The two women looked at Concha. The terrified girl shook her head yes. No man was brave enough to approach her. They were afraid of Ixma's wrath.

"Good," the witch said. "Then her virginity will go for a handsome price."

"Katna pushed Concha toward the witch. Then Katna asked the witch what she needed to do to find the magician of Tikal. The witch gave Katna detailed instructions for finding the wizard who could give her son immortality.

"It took three months for him to come to Uxmal. Katna had been told that the price for his work was to be her life. When he arrived, Katna was ordered to bring her son to the Pyramid of the Magician at sunset. They went into a secret chamber within the pyramid. There the conversion began. It is there that Ixma stays to this day."

"Concha did not know exactly what happened within that room. Later, when she was reunited with Ixma, he told her something of the surgery that lasted four days. Ixma related that all his eternal organs were removed and replaced with hundreds of little crystals that were the size of a chick pea. The part of the body where the crystals were stored was kept secret by Ixma."

"After the surgery was complete, it was time to activate the crystals. It was also time for Katna to surrender her life. Ixma related how the sorcerer then had Katna stand in front of him. He grabbed her and pressed his lips to hers. He made three almost inaudible sounds and then began to suck. In a few minutes Katna's body was now shriveled beyond recognition. Next the sorcerer gave Ixma the life force he had just taken from his mother. Ixma had to put his lips on the sorcerer's in order to receive the life force. There was a second set of three sounds that needs to be made to give life force to another."

"The conjuror then gave Ixma his bittersweet news. The life force of one person would only energize the crystals for a three-month period. Then he would have to find another victim. He could only leave his resting place four times a year, at the time of the solstices and the equinoxes. He could travel through the dark portals to the upper world and the Underworld only on these days, when the energy of the planet is at its peak.

The master magician gave Ixma other gifts. One is that his is able to project an image of the way he wants other to see him to one or many people at once. As long as he maintains his focus, this image will hold. This gives him enough time to attract a woman to kiss. He also received protective symbols, embroidered on an enchanted cloth that he must use during his sleep time. This cloth contains a powerful spell. When the sorcerer was done with his work, he covered Ixma with the cloth of protection, and then he was left alone."

"Time passed. Concha was old and of no use to the witch. The witch told Concha where her brother was, and cast her out of Chichen Itza. She had a dream that Ixma want to see her. Concha said they had a connection that allowed them to communicate through dreams. She made her way to the chamber and was reunited with her extraordinary brother. When Ixma gave Concha the life force the first time, it rejuvenated all the cells in her body and made her look like she does today."

On solstice and equinox days, he would go through the portal to a place that he named Boca Negra. At that time, it was just a beach. Concha said that he would prey on the village whores at first. Then Concha had to scout out victims for him. Finding one that would not be missed was her job."

"Now Concha is Ixma's link to the outside world. It was during the 1950's that Concha had the idea of getting money for making rich women disappear. Ixma's money built the structures that are Boca Negra today. Many tycoons from the United States came to Mexico at that time. Concha was in a position to meet them and suggest the option that she had for them. These rich men from the US were now able to dispose of mistresses who had become problematic, and wives who wanted too much alimony. Concha has benefited from the money that has come from this travesty. Maybe you have come to put an end to all of this," Felipe said as he brought his story to a close.

"This is so bizarre that it must be true," Morgan stated softly.

"I hope you understand now why Concha must supply YOUR dead body to those that paid to have it. Concha has already spent their money. It appears your husband is one of the richest and most influential spouses who have ever used this service. He must be appeased. Otherwise the business will end. Ixma can only come out at the Spring Equinox. It is then that you must do battle with him. You will have to vanquish him through playing the Mayan handball game."

"Handball!" Morgan exclaimed "My life depends on a game???"

"Yes, I am afraid so. If you were to escape, Ixma could find you by using the other dark portals that are all over the planet. Then he could surprise you and you would have no chance against him."

"What a mess I am in!" Morgan wailed.

"Don't worry. You will be prepared. You will have to dig deep inside yourself for this challenge.

93

You have not done anything like this before. You have been called into action. Ixma must be stopped. His carnage of helpless women puts murderers like Jack the Ripper to shame. I feel that you have been called to fulfill a destiny. You must be a warrior, whether you know it or not."

This last statement caused Morgan to whine emphatically. "I am not a warrior. I am an ex-trophy wife who can't even balance a check book. I have done nothing for the last nine years but work out and shop! "

"Calm yourself, Morgan. I have more to tell you. We are coming into shore. Concha is waiting for you. I want you to know that I am on your side. I will help you behind Concha's back. I must tell her about your heritage. Your husband now knows that you are alive. He has given Concha Carte Blanche to do what she wants with you. All he wants is your dead body washed up on shore, so that you look like you drowned yourself. Concha has assured your husband that he will have your body on March 22nd." In order for Ixma to leave his cavern, they have to wait until March 21st, the Spring Equinox. On the Equinox, as you have seen, the portal can expand to encompass a large area. The Maya knew that the power of the planet could be harnessed during those four days each year."

"The official story that I am supposed to tell you is: due to your crazy, life-threatening behavior at the Solstice party, your husband is concerned for your safety. There were many witnesses that saw you running around the beach, chasing what seemed like the air. That is also part of the program. The Atole makes the victim look like they are delusional to witnesses. Concha wants you to think that you have no legal rights, and that you are in a make-shift mental hospital, getting therapy for your behavior. There will be a guard outside your room at all times. You will be in my care the rest of the time. If I were to let you escape, they would kill my family. She wants you to think that after you have shown her that you are able to play the game, you will be permitted to go back to the language school for the spring quarter and go on as if nothing has happened."

After hearing this story, Morgan contemplated how deep the water was as they got into the harbor, and the ferry slowly made its way to the dock. "Too deep to swim. That is not my strong sport," she thought.

"You cannot escape this, Morgan." Felipe said. Morgan sat up straight after he said those words. She was in shock that he seemed to have read her thoughts. "Just play dumb. I have told you the truth, the whole story. I have already risked my life and the lives of my relatives to help you. Do what I tell you to do and you will come out of this alive. The only way out is though, Morgan." The engine of the ferry had now slowed to an idle as it met with the dock at Playa Del Carmen. Concha was waiting, with her two lovers, at the entrance to the ferry.

"Hello my dear," Concha said as she approached her. "We are so happy to see you."

Morgan suddenly received the mental image of Concha salivating and licking her lips, as the smiling woman walked toward her. Morgan had already decided to play dumb. The first thing Morgan said after she shook Concha's warm, soft hand was "I want to talk to my lawyers."

Concha and Felipe laughed loudly. "He is playing dumb too, I guess," Morgan thought. Concha rattled off a monologue in Spanish that Felipe translated. He knew that Enrique understood English, so Felipe was careful to translate what Concha said and with a tone of voice that would show his respect for her.

"She said that is impossible. We are going back to Concha's house. She has a lovely room ready for you. Concha wonders if you would like a hot bath and something hot to eat." When Felipe said this, he gave Morgan a look that was the Universal sign for "Don't be stupid, you had better be humble and say OK."

"OK." Morgan replied and then lowered her head in a sign of submission. She was basically told to shut up. Concha was in her power now. She was putting out a lot of force. Morgan could feel it coming from her. "She must have had a yummy dinner of young women," Morgan thought as she recalled all that Felipe had shared on the ferry.

Mama Mia

As Morgan and Felipe approached the entrance to Morgan's new home, they could see a rotund, balding Mexican man who was sitting in a chair near the door. Leaning up against the chair was a rifle. As Morgan entered the room, she got the impression that the room had once been part of a downstairs garage.

"Don't react, Morgan" Felipe whispered as he took her by the arm and opened the door of the room for her. "Do not try to leave the room without me. If you need me for something, tell the man outside. You just have to say my name, FELIPE, and they will call me. Give that Irish temper a rest. I will see you tomorrow. Pleasant dreams." He gave Morgan one of his great, ice-melting smiles as he closed the door. The room was clean and very nicely furnished with wicker and rattan. It was on the bottom level of the modern, split-level house, underneath a big deck that looked out at the ocean. The color scheme was royal blue and tan. The décor had a Caribbean feel more than a brightly colored traditional Mexican color scheme.

The side of the room that faced the ocean was comprised of sliding glass doors and windows that had padlocks on the exteriors. The room was about 60 feet above the sand so the locks could only be reached with the help of a tall ladder. "Escaping out the window is not looking good." Morgan decided as she examined them more closely. The room had a bed, desk, television and chairs. There was a plate of fish covered in a red salsa and a bowl of fruit. There were also bars of chocolate, different types of pastries and carafes filled with water and colored liquids.

"SHOWER" was the word that came into her mind first. Somehow water was now very important to her. "I need to submerge myself in water. That will make everything better and may even make this nightmare go away." Even though Morgan said this to herself, she knew that this was not a dream. The guard outside the door was a big dose of reality. She shed her clothes quickly and left her tote bag on the table near the food. She took a short shower and then got out and filled the tub with steaming water. She had to soak herself in it. When she got in the tub, she closed her eyes and laid her head back. She just wanted to relax and mentally get away from the strange mess she seemed to be in. In a few moments all the thoughts about the night in the Underworld, with the brawny dancer, came back. She remembered his cold hands, and the thought sent shivers down her spine. "A midget!" she exclaimed as she felt her muscles beginning to relax. It all seemed all like a dream. Morgan was beginning to let her body rest after the long ordeal that she had been through.

After 25 minutes in the tub had passed and Morgan felt revived, she started to get out. She did feel much better being in the water. She realized she enjoyed the water more than she ever had. "Must be the Playa Del Carmen water," she thought and chuckled to herself. After she had warped herself in the luxurious robe that waited on a hook by the tub, she came back to the bedroom with one thought on her mind: food. She heated up a waiting plate of food in the nearby microwave and sat down to a savory Mexican meal. The seasoning was perfect for Morgan. It was spicy but not too hot. "They have a very good cook," the captive decided. All of this was, of course, mind chatter that kept Morgan distracted from thinking about the validity of her situation.

While she was picking at her fish and trying to comb the knots out of her hair, another thought came to her: Escape. It took only a few minutes for a plan to hatch within Morgan's mind. "I am going to wait until the middle of the night, and then I will take the screen off of the little bathroom window and jump onto the sand. It's only about 60 ft. down. The bottom is sand, so it should break my fall. Then I can hitchhike into town. I will wait until I hear the guard snoring. I still have my wallet and passport in my purse. This break out can work," she told herself as she tested the liquids in the carafes and found the clear to be water.

She downed several glasses and after that got back to her thoughts of escape. She dug into her purse to find the passport and after that her hands rested on the picture of Gerard. The glass was cracked, but he was still smiling and holding up that fish. Shock and disbelief came flooding into her mind. "How could you want to kill me?" she thought. "It was the money, and your father who never liked me, of course." Morgan felt that his family was behind this. They felt she was too common for him.

Then she realized that she was getting caught up in sorting this all out. "It doesn't matter. I am going to get out of here and get back to the US. Still too early to go," she thought as she looked at the sunset that was in full bloom. "I'll take a nap until it's time to go," she said to herself as she walked to the bed. She did not get under the covers. She did not want to sleep long.

Shortly after she stretched out on the bed and closed her eyes, she heard a voice calling "Moorrrgan" in velvety tones. The voice was gentle and loving. Morgan knew that she was not asleep. She kept her eyes closed and started to sit up. "Moorrrgan" the voice said again. When Morgan sat up and open her eyes, she saw what Felipe had described: an incredibly sexual woman with lengthy, dark ringlets of hair that looked like they were floating in water and huge green eyes. Her lips were blood red, and her breasts barely stayed inside her form fitting, floor length, tattered black dress. Morgan's first impression: Felipe was right: Elvira with big hair.

"Hello my dear. So good to see you again"

Morgan was in shock. She pinched herself to make sure she was not asleep. "I am wide awake with Elvira hovering in front of me. What next???" she thought to herself. In a quiet, polite tone of voice Morgan stated, "I am sorry. I don't believe we have ever met."

That statement evoked a blood chilling laugh.

"What is so funny?" Morgan thought to herself. Now the lanky beauty was getting a bit scared. "How did you get in here?" Morgan asked, taking the offensive. Big mistake. Suddenly the woman expanded to the height of the whole room. Her eyes flared green flames, and she started to hiss. "Ok," Morgan thought, "now I am really scared.' Another terrifying laugh.

"Oh Morgan, don't be scared." The she-devil's voice was soft and soothing again. She had now shrunk to Morgan's height. "I am not going to hurt you. I need you. I have work for you to do. I know your every thought, Morgan. I know that you are planning to flee from this place, but that would be very foolish." Her eyes flared with emerald flames. "You cannot escape me, Morgan O'Neil. Your soul has been pledged to me for eternity. You were one of my priestesses when we first met in Ireland. Your mother, who is your mother in this life, was dying. You prayed to me to restore her health. You made a vow to serve me if I healed you mother. I answered your prayer, and your mother was spared for another seven years. You left your family and came to live in my temple. You were instructed in the ways of a priestess and carried out many duties for me. Now it is time for you to do that again."

Morgan was beyond freaked out. She was in a state of panic. She ran for the door. The woman appeared in front of her, blocked the door and had a wicked yet serene look on her face. "If you try to leave I will find you and torment you beyond belief for rest of this life and for all your other lives to come."

"Whoa, let's start over." Morgan said. She was not the first person that thought they could bargain with supernatural forces. "I can see that we have gotten off on the wrong foot. Please calm down. OK. I get It. I see I can't escape this. I really can't relate to the 'priestess in another life' thing. Maybe you can explain a bit more about that to me. Right now, I don't know what is the lesser of the two evils: the midget magician or you."

"He is merely a fly on the wall. I am ancient Ireland's goddess of Sex, Death, War, Prophecy and Vengeance: The Morrighan. I have helped the Irish kings of old win battles if they became my lovers. I have shown myself to those who will die in battle. I am the goddess of fertility. I appear to the mother in her dreams and announce the coming of a child. I have many powers that you cannot comprehend in your human state. My priestesses have been carrying out my desires for countless centuries. Now it is time for you to do my bidding."

"Your bidding?" Morgan questioned in a polite tone.

"You must do away with that filthy parasite of a man, the supposed magician who has been slaughtering innocent woman for many years. You must annihilate him."

"Now I don't mean to be disrespectful," Morgan quickly stated, " Why do you need me? You seem to be pretty formidable, by the looks of things." Morgan was thinking that flattery might get her somewhere.

"My dear, I can read every thought you have. I appreciate your kindness, but I know that you still desire to escape this challenge. Nevertheless, you cannot." The Morrighan smiled and sent a wave of pain through Morgan's body. Morgan sunk to the floor and landed in the fetal position. She was helpless to free her from the stinging, burning pain that was surging through her body. Morgan opened her eyes and could see that she was covered with green flames. There was no real fire.

"Stop, please! I am burning to a crisp!" Morgan screamed out in her mind. In what seemed like days, but was really only minutes, the stinging stopped. The Morrighan chuckled a bit. She then hovered over Morgan's limp body. The specter floated around the room while she talked to a whimpering Morgan, who lay quivering on the floor.

"I cannot go into the place where this mutant will be. As a human in a physical body, only you can go to the place they call the Underworld. You must vanquish him so that he will not take the lives of women. Many children have not been able to come into this world because of all the women he has killed. His actions have created an imbalance in the forces of life and death. Vengeance must be done. He must be stopped. You have been called forth into service to address this issue. "

"This is all so strange. I feel like my life is in shambles." Morgan stated with a bit of a whimper in her voice.

"My dear," the giant Elvira stated," Your life will never be the same. Long ago you pledged yourself to my service, and now you must do as I desire. You cannot escape. You have no free will. You surrendered that to me long ago. You could have escaped this fate you now face. You had until your 30th birthday to produce a female child with a mate from our ancient blood line. That would have spared you from this obligation. That is how your mother and grandmother avoided being called to duty. A priestess of The Morrighan must either produce a child who could be called into service, or do battle herself. You have chosen the second option." With this, The Morrighan floated around the room, cackling.

"Due to the fact that you married into the family of our old enemies, you were prevented from conceiving. The French have done battle with the Irish since ancient times. You were a pawn in their game from the beginning. Our adversaries wanted you to have a child with Gerard. That would have destroyed our blood line and taken away our magic. I could not allow that to happen. I was there every time you engaged with Gerard. I made sure that no child would emerge from your womb."

"Even though you were not aware of this situation in your conscious mind, part of you did know this man was not right for you. You did not heed the Quiet

Voice. It told you not to marry him. The guides and teachers from the higher realms use a soft, yet clear whisper to assist humans on this planet. Yet you were dazzled by his excessive lifestyle and did not listen to the warning of the little voice inside that told that he was not proper for you. Your choice of a mate shamed me and your roots." The Morrighan's eyes flared. Morgan braced herself for more pain that thankfully did not come. The Morrighan's words went deep into Morgan's spirit. She said nothing. "You lay in bed with our foe. I could not allow you to bear an offspring. Your actions forced you into the path of the warrior priestess. Your life's mission is now to serve me as a soldier for my causes. It has been this way since the Irish created me, many centuries ago. Their prayers and pleas for help on the battlefield brought me into existence. Now I am powerful beyond belief, as more and more take on the old ways again and hold me in their thoughts."

The Morrighan floated around the room again, as if lost in thought. "You could have been open to a man from your heritage and been free of the pledge to do battle in my name. He would have come, as he did for your mother. You allowed yourself to be swept away by money and earthly power. Now you must pay the price. " The Morrighan continued floating around the room. Morgan started to shake out of fear.

"You will be prepared well for this battle." The Morrighan stated, as she sensed Morgan's fear. "The protection that saved you from the repulsive little man was put in place by your grandmother. Your mother helped as well, but it was your grandmother who was able to manifest the Orb of Protection. She was not only a great priestess but a great conjuror in her own right. I could have stopped her, but I let her have her way with this. Your grandmother also put the Seal of the House of O'Neil within you. If you are able to uphold this ancient pact, and bring honor to your clan, the seal will come out upon the surface of your body. It is a mark of respect and ability that many of your house received in the times long gone. The O'Neil clan always had great ability with the magic arts. Your grandmother was one of the best." With that The Morrighan let out another horrific cackle. "The protection could only be used once. Now you must go into battle unprotected. If you do not succeed, you will be lost in the Underworld. Do not sniffle or grovel. It is so unbecoming of your new position." The Morrighan let out another blooding curdling laugh. Morgan was overwhelmed; tears had started to stream down her face.

"No offence, but you said that you were the goddess of prophecy. Can't you tell how this turns out?" Morgan said in a pleading tone.

"I told you that my ability cannot work in the Underworld. I have no power there. You can go there because you have a human body. That is why you are obliged to go. You must go forward in confidence. The fighter is within you. Now it is time for it to emerge."

"I see that resistance is pointless," Morgan thought to herself as she stood up. Morgan had a flash go through her mind that The Morrighan would pursue her and torment her if she did not comply. Then Morgan realized that The Morrighan was showing her a picture of what would happen if Morgan defied her. After a short moment, Morgan said, "I will do what you ask. I will stay and fight this magician. Then I can be free to have my own life?"

"You have gone through a change in your body chemistry. I have awakened your bond with water. You have been given the ability to derive strength from the water. We must always be around water. That is now a source of power. It can give you strength and skill that is beyond the abilities of a normal human body. You must have noticed that already" The Morrighan stated.

Morgan did notice that The Morrighan did not answer her last question. Morgan also sensed that she should not push for more right now. "Well I have to admit that I do feel the energy from the water," she responded. Morgan realized that it was best to comply.

"Lie on the bed" the Phantom Queen of Ireland commanded. Morgan timidly went to the bed and lay on her back. Morgan felt a slight pressure on her face. Then she felt that she was plunging into a pool of water, yet she felt that her body was dry. Scenes started to appear through her mind's eye. Morgan saw herself as a skinny, down trodden young girl, maybe 18; who went into a stone building that Morgan sensed was a temple. There she saw herself, in a past life, kneel before the altar and pledge her soul to the service of the goddess Morrighan. Green flames suddenly covered the girl. They seemed to burn away her sadness. After the flames subsided, Morgan saw the girl transformed into a healthy, radiant priestess. Next, scenes of the service that Morgan had done for the goddess flashed before her. First, Morgan saw herself making love to a man in the fields during feast day. This was when the goddess allowed humans to merge with her and produce offspring. The next scene was that of a battle. Men were fighting; Morgan was taking care of the wounded. Next she saw herself in the temple, allowing the energy of The Morrighan to come through her hands to the sick that needed healing. Then the scenes disappeared. Morgan felt the pressure on her body lift. She could open her eyes and sit up.

"How incredible!" Morgan said to the deity. The scenes were humbling to Morgan. They showed her a life very unlike the indulgent one she had known with Gerard. It was a life of service to others. Morgan also felt that a transformation was taking place in her subconscious. She said to The Morrighan, "I know that I had a very different existence at other times. I am getting the sense that what you have just shared with me is opening me to a new direction. I feel that you have triggered something within me that has been asleep. Even though this is all so weird, I feel that what is happening is right for me. It will be interesting to see how the past will manifest in this present time. I understand now that being of service is very rewarding emotionally. I know now why I am the one to stop the magician."

"You have very talented helpers. The man who is assisting you was an Irish physician who tended to the wounded in battle. He comes from a line of great kings. He will make you ready to win this battle. Do not fear. Do not doubt. Think VICTORY and you will have it. Now sleep." Suddenly, Morgan felt herself pushed down on the bed. Sleep came immediately.

Moonlight Stroll

Morgan had slept for almost a day. When she awoke, it was nearly dusk again. She decided to partake of her favorite activity: a shower. When she was drying off, she heard a knock at the door. "Just a minute" she yelled.

"It is Felipe. I will wait until you are dressed. Then I need to come in to talk to you. Concha sent me."

Morgan opened the closet to see if there were any clothes. Her old clothes were gone. She found a long, white Mexican Wedding dress with embroidered flowers around the neck. She threw it over her body and yelled" Come in"

Felipe opened the door and sat down at the table. "It is as I hoped. Concha has asked me to deal with you, mainly, because I speak English. She also has an idea that you may find me attractive. She wants us to be lovers. She feels that will help you trust me. Concha does view the world in terms of sex. She is an expert in that area."

"I really don't know who to trust. The Elvira chick paid me a visit last night. She wants me to destroy the magician. Is he really a midget? He looked so hot that night." After she said that, she looked to Felipe, who was sending her the international signal for "Why don't you let that go?"

"He is not a man; he is not even human. You must execute him when the time comes. Concha does not suspect that I am sympatric to your cause. It is Christmas Eve. She would like us to attend a fiesta, right outside on the beach. We still have much to discuss, and I thought that might be entertaining."

"What the hell," Morgan said. "Will there be beer there?"

"Of course. There will also be wine and even Irish Whisky if you desire!" Felipe replied. "The neighborhood is making a big bond fire. No one will be able to see your face clearly, but you must keep the hood up on your sweatshirt."

She found some jeans and a sweatshirt with a hood that were in the closet. They fit her fairly well. Mexican sandals with tire soles were in there as well.

"OK. Ready." Morgan stated. He held open the door to the outside. Once outside, Morgan could see the bonfire. It was a few hundred feet away. Felipe made a gesture to the guard outside the door, and escorted Morgan to the sand.

There were many people around the vicinity of the fire. As they got closer to the fire, Felipe said, "Keep your head down and the hood pulled over your face. You don't want people looking at you." Morgan did as she was instructed. Felipe put his arm around her shoulder to guide her through the crowd of people they were approaching. They walked by a table where the beer was. There were also many bottles of wine and hard liquor on display. After that table, there was one that had slabs of cooked meat that were being meticulously sliced. Next to the platters of shredded meat were tortillas, rolls and the fixings for tacos or sandwiches. Morgan poured herself a glass of beer and smiled broadly at Felipe.

"I have what I want." Morgan said happily.

"I will get the tacos" Felipe chuckled. "You need to eat something." He kept an eye on her as he quickly filled two plates with ready-made tacos. When he returned with the full plates of food, Felipe led the way to some rocks that were away from the crowd and close to the water. Morgan sat down and started to take in deep breaths. The sea air felt better to her then she could ever remember. 'Maybe The Morrighan was right about the water. I do feel much better being close to it," Morgan thought.

She put the plate of food on her lap and started to sip her beer.

"Eat some food. You will need your strength. You have time off tomorrow. It is Christmas. The day after, you will start your training. You will meet with me and Lupe. Lupe is an herbalist. She made the tea that you were drinking before you arrived in the Yucatan as well as the potion in the Atole. The tea was designed to block your psychic abilities. That way, you would not know what was coming."

This last bit of info enraged Morgan so much, that she put her beer down, stood up with her plate of food and was about to hurl it. Felipe made a last minute interception before the plate of food was pitched into the sand. "I have been drugged since the beginning of the divorce?" Morgan's angry whisper came through clinched teeth.

Felipe had to work really hard to get out of the hole he had just dug for himself. "You did have your inner guidance working." Felipe piped in. He was going to turn this around for her. "Something caused you to stop taking the tea before you got to Boca Negra. Your intuition must have still been working, in spite of the situation. You are one hell of a woman, Morgan!" Felipe's plan worked and Morgan smiled, sat down and got back to her second beer. Felipe let out a quiet sigh of relief. "Keeping her in line is a big job" he thought to himself. "Yet she is so precious; I don't mind." A slight smile came over his face as he started to ingest his meal. There was a silence as Morgan drank and Felipe ate. After she made her way through the beer, she started to look at her plate of food with interest. That brought another grin to Felipe's face.

"You must eat. You are now going into a rigorous training period the day-after tomorrow." He watched with a joy that surprised him as she started to eat her taco. After she had polished off a couple of them, Felipe felt it was safe to start again on the information he needed to share. "Even though she is a bit tipsy, her subconscious will take in all that I am saying. She will wake up tomorrow with an understanding of the situation," he thought encouragingly to himself, as he proceeded on.

"Lupe also made the drink that took you to the Underworld that night." The beer had done its job, and Morgan did not react to this last statement. "She is only doing what Ixma and Concha desire. If not her, someone else would have made the potions. Lupe will help you succeed because she is my relative and in agreement with your purpose." After a moment of quiet reflection, Morgan shook her head in agreement. She didn't want to hold on to resentment about someone she had not yet met. Then she held out an empty beer glass and gave Felipe a big smile. He immediately understood the International signal for "More beer, please!" When he returned with a frothy glass of the golden beverage, he felt that it was safe to continue.

"You will have to take the potion in order to learn to move in the Underworld. This is critical to preparing for the final handball game. The potion that you will get will not be as strong as the one you took on the solstice. Then you will be able to learn how to move in the Underworld. As you may have realized, the Underworld is all around us. It is a different frequency. It is all right here, right now. You have to get used to the weightlessness of your body when in the Underworld. It is a bit like floating in a space ship. The Maya used plant medicine for many things. They used the plants to heal the body, and they used it to take themselves to the other dimensions."

"What is in the drink that takes you to the Underworld?" Morgan wondered aloud.

"It is a combination of a few different herbs, but mostly what you in the United States call the Magic Mushrooms."

That phrase made Morgan laugh. "I took some of those when I was in high school."

"Yes, many use the herbs for fun and to have great sex!" Felipe said, and they both had a good laugh. Morgan was nodding and laughing freely. Felipe realized that his feelings slipped out with that last comment. He had to watch that, he felt. "I find it interesting that you have taken the sacred mushrooms before," he said, bowing his head in thought for a moment. "It must mean that you were meant to do this. There are usually signs in a person's life that will show them glimpses of their destiny before it happens. I feel taking the mushrooms before this time is a sign that you were destined to be here and experience this challenge."

This last statement caused Morgan to let out a large sigh. "Destined to do this. This is a hard pill to swallow, but I guess that I am." Morgan stated solemnly and then turned to face Felipe.

A thought of joy bubbled up from Felipe's mind. "She is finally accepting her fate."

"The Morrighan paid me a visit last night," Morgan continued. "That is her name. I do think that

115

Elvira Babe is more suited to her. She said that I had to face this challenge, or she would harass me for eternity," Morgan said in a serious tone. "She was pretty intense. She gave me a sample of the pain I was in for if I didn't comply," Morgan added. There was no anger in her voice, just acceptance.

"She is very powerful," Felipe nodded in agreement.

"She said that she didn't create that protective field that saved me from Ixma. She said that my dead grandma made it for me."

Felipe seemed very impressed. "You can only stop magic with magic. You have great magic within you, Morgan. You just haven't gotten in touch with it. The time has come for you to step into your gifts."

As Felipe was eating his dinner, Morgan moved closer to him. Even though she was feeling the effects of the beer, she was still fairly clear in the head. "What is it that you do for Concha and Ixma?" Morgan asked in a quiet tone of voice.

"When Ixma sucks the life force out of a woman's body, the soul is left behind. The majority of the time the souls remain in the Underworld. They are trapped there. They cannot go through the portal without a human body. They usually cannot come out into this world so that they can go to The Light, The Source. Returning to Source is the natural next step for the soul when the human body is no longer of service. Every now and again, a soul gets through the black portal in the Underworld and ends up at Boca Negra. It is one of the amazing aspects of the spirit. When the soul body is somehow able to get out through the black portal, it ends up wandering around the beach, looking for the way back to the Light. They appear as ghosts to living humans. There are people that are on the lookout for such an event. They also work for Concha. She does not want any messy situations going on that would put a damper on her business. Concha doesn't need any ghosts hovering around Boca Negra, warning the next victims or just bothering the people that live nearby.

That is when they ask me to go to work. I find the lost soul; I talk to it, heal it and send it back to the Light." Felipe was silent for a moment. He felt the heaviness of the situation on his shoulders. "It is a great travesty, this state of affairs. The misplaced souls cannot find tranquility or respite. They move constantly through the Underworld. This is the part that is a great disgrace to me. Every soul deserves rest when it leaves the body, not endless torment. The dead must be allowed to find peace."

"Now I understand why this is so important." Morgan said. "If I can end their suffering, then I must do it." She sat up straight, put her hands on her knees, took in a deep breath and let it out slowly.

"Morgan, you have the heart of a warrior. What you just said is imperative to the success of this mission. You need to have compassion for the innocent women who are still suffering from succumbing to Ixma's lust and Concha's greed."

Felipe stopped eating his taco and looked at her for a long minute. "I guess you do have something inside you besides looking for the right pair of shoes," he said with a chuckle.

Morgan laughed in agreement. "That was the life I got used to living. I was a poor college girl when I met Gerard. My mother and grandmother raised me in a very sparse environment. We had very little, but we always had food and shelter. My needs were unfailingly met, even if I didn't grow up wearing designer outfits," Morgan said with a twinge of pride as she thought of the women who raised her. "Why do you think that I was so taken with Gerard? It was the money, as well as his great ass!" Morgan said with a laugh. "Seriously, I was swayed by the money. I grew up a street smart, wisecracking teenager. The wealth was phenomenal. When that world started to fall apart, I realized that I didn't want the money, I cared about him. Now, after finding all this out, I don't know why I agonized about him so much." Morgan stated in an emotionless tone. "Now I seem to be starting out on another life. This new existence seems to be based on righting wrongs and being of service. The Morrighan probably has much for me to do," Morgan said as an afterthought.

"The agreement you made with her in a past life is binding you now. Try to think of it this way," Felipe said, flashing that grin that Morgan thought could melt snow; it made him look so hot. "You are coming to see your true nature. I also feel that something inside of you wanted this outcome. Who you are in this life is an avenger, not a mother. The Morrighan is helping you to fulfill your potential. I feel that this challenge only activated you for your new path, a path that deep down, you really want to walk," he added politely.

"I am on the way to becoming a slimy midget killer!" she howled with laughter. The alcohol and the nurturing ocean breeze were encouraging Morgan to express herself. She finished her beer and then smiled demurely at Felipe, "Want to take a walk down the beach?" she asked, gesturing with her head to a deserted stretch of beach. It did not take a psychic to tell that the tone in her voice was more than a bit alluring.

Felipe thought for a moment and then said, "Why don't we walk on the beach this way?" he pointed to the area that was dimly illumined with Christmas lights. Morgan got up, with a smile on her face that said "busted" After they arrived on the wet sand, Felipe was the first to talk.

"I am supposed to be inquisitive about your upbringing. Concha wants to know how that green force field came up. Now I can tell her that it was put in place at birth by a dead relative. Then they will drop the issue. If someone was going to come to your rescue and whisk you away, it would have happened by now. It seems that The Morrighan wants to do the opposite: keep you here."

Morgan nodded in agreement. "I haven't a clue as to how the force field worked," Morgan said honestly.

"I know that my mother and grandmother were always brewing up something. They had a lot of herbs, statues, crystals, animal parts and incense hanging around. Mom and grandma often did ceremonies on the full moon and the new moon. I never participated. "Morgan caught herself as she remembered one occasion that happened when she had her first menstrual cycle. " Well, when I got my first period, my mother and grandma just went psycho. When I showed my mother the pool of blood that I awoke to, she started to jump for joy. She and Grandma thought it was great. My stomach hurt, and I didn't appreciate all the hoopla."

"We have similar ceremonies when a girl becomes a woman. There are big celebrations, feasting and dancing." Felipe added.

"As I remember, it was not much fun. My grandma had me lie down naked on the beach at midnight, and the two of them started to sing and dance around me. Then mother covered me with a green paste. That was weird. They gave me two stones to hold, one in each hand. At the end of the ceremony, they told me to go wash off in the ocean and throw the stones in the water. That whole thing was a drag because it was December. I was freezing! I had to stay in the ocean until grandma said I could come out. All, in all, it was a very peculiar experience. I was glad when it was all over. I did feel different after. Now that I think about it, I did have a really unusual dream that night." Morgan got a strange look on her face. "Wow! I just now realized

120

that The Morrighan was in the dream. She gave me an emerald that went right into my forehead. Then she kissed me on the cheek and cackled that malicious laugh."

"It seems that The Morrighan has been a guardian to you throughout your life. She has probably been watching over you from birth." Felipe chimed in.

"She certainly has," Morgan thought as she remembered that the Morrighan kept her from conceiving a child. "Are you going to tell Concha all about me?"

"I am not going to tell them everything, just what they might find interesting. She will be suspicious if I don't tell her something. The Coming of Age ceremony that you have described is interesting. It is good for them to know that The Morrighan is your protector in this world. It will keep them from trying anything underhanded before the handball game. Any trickery would leave them open for reprisals. What you have told me will not give Ixma an advantage over you. They just want to know who they are dealing with. Clearly you, yourself, do not know what you can do. I have nothing to hide from them at the moment. It will be interesting to see what emerges from within you." He gave her a smile that felt, to Morgan, like a teacher speaking to a new pupil. "What you have told me will satisfy Concha's curiosity and will pacify Ixma. From what I know of ancient magic, the green light that protected you is a classic example of a protection spell. It will probably not protect you again. I have been told that a spell like that usually only works one time," he stated.

"You are right about that." Morgan quickly added. "My grandmother told me that it could not work again. So did The Morrighan."

"I do know that Ixma is terrified of The Morrighan. Ixma seems to know that she can't go to the Underworld. He feels that if he challenges you to a game of handball, in the Underworld, he can win the right to sacrifice your body and soul to the Lords of Night. He also feels safe there. The Lords of Night just want your head. The Maya considered the skull the symbol of immortality. An ancient legend tells of the vast collection of skulls that the Lords of Night have in the Underworld. This is why you must learn to successfully take part in the handball game. You don't want yours to be part of the collection! My job is to teach you how to be in motion in the Underworld and how to play the sport."

"Well, I don't have any other pressing engagements at the time," Morgan said with a chuckle.

They walked on in silence for a time. Then Felipe said, "Don't worry, Morgan, you will have another chance to find true love."

Morgan stared at him with a penetrating gaze. "How do you know that? Are you getting some premonition? Do you see that in my future?" she asked eagerly.

Felipe laughed and then said, "I feel your loneliness. You are a stunning woman, Morgan. You will find another man. Many men if you like." He let out a large laugh. "Next time choose wisely. Don't go for the money or even the looks, like you did before. You have to choose a man by looking at what is in his heart. Let your intuition tell you what he feels for you. That is the factor that is most important. You will find a man that cares about you completely."

"I hope you are right" Morgan said with a hopeful tone in her voice.

"Now is not the time to think of men. At present, it is the time to rest and learn how to survive in the Underworld of the Maya," he added.

While they talked, walked and enjoyed the cool evening breeze, Felipe realized that they were getting too far away and that it was time to return Morgan to her quarters. They turned around and were soon close to Concha's house. They both recognized that it was now the moment for Felipe to escort her to the front door of her room. Morgan felt some fear and sadness as she realized that she had to go back to the reality of her unusual situation. She was already beginning to think of it as a prison cell. They walked up to the entrance, and he opened the door. "Sleep well tonight. You will be coming to the fiesta tomorrow night. There will be piñatas, music and much more. It will be fun. You will get to know something of our customs. Sleep well."

"Hopefully The Morrighan will not show up tonight," Morgan reflected as Felipe backed out of the doorway and closed the door. She quickly took off her clothes and got under the covers. "I just want to have a good night's sleep." Morgan looked up at the ceiling, and then around the empty room. She felt that she was saying that to the bevy of unseen guests, including her grandmother and The Morrighan. "They are probably hovering around the room," she thought and then giggled. Morgan blew all the unseen visitors a big kiss and got comfortable. She slept profoundly well.

Merry Christmas

Morgan awoke to the sounds of very loud Mexican music. After a few moments, she realized it was Jose Faliciano singing Feliz Navidad. "Well, it must be Christmas." Morgan thought as she got up and went right into the shower. She enjoyed the warm water pouring over her. Then, what Felipe said the night before came flooding back. "I guess I need to get up and get some Christmas cheer," she thought as she tried to block out what awaited her in the future. "I am not fighting him to day," Morgan told herself as she was washing her hair. "Let's not get bummed out so early in the day. I have almost three months to get ready. Don't worry now," she thought as she started to get out of the shower. After she dried off, she found all that she needed to look like she had slept in a bed and not on a street corner.

Just then there was a knock on the door. Morgan went to the door, wrapped in a towel, and opened it. A very attractive Mexican man, in his early twenties, was standing outside with a covered plate of food. "Good morning" he said in a cheerful tone of voice. "I am Enrique. I am at your service. Here is some breakfast for you. Merry Christmas."

"Gracias" Morgan decided to return the favor of speaking his native tongue. He handed her the plate and then backed away from the door. Morgan was left alone to eat her breakfast. She was still a bit groggy from the beer of the night before and from the whole adventure in general.

She ate her breakfast and then decided that she was going to do some yoga. She got down on the floor and started to do some yoga positions. This always made her feel good. After going through her favorite dozen poses, Morgan felt tired. She decided to crawl back into bed.

When she awoke, she could see the apricot streaks of clouds that made her realize it was sunset. She sat up, stretched and decided to get out of bed. There were a few magazines next to the night stand. All of a sudden, she had the desire to look around for her purse. "I want to find my passport," Morgan thought to herself. For some strange reason, she felt the need to locate it. She found her purse and began to rummage through it. She started to dig frantically as she realized that her passport was not in the place she thought it would be. Then the light bulb went on. "They went through my purse while I was asleep!" Everything was there except the passport and the wallet.

So many emotions were going through her as she went to the nightstand and looked at Gerard's picture. Now she knew the truth. She was irate, miserable and anxious. Part of her wanted to throw the picture on the ground and stomp all over it. Morgan had an overwhelming desire to tear his likeness into tiny pieces. Just as she picked up the framed picture with the broken glass, ready to destroy it in some way, she heard the Quiet Voice inside. It said, "No, don't throw him away just yet." Morgan shook her head, as if something was stuck in her ear. Now that Morgan knew where the voice originated from, she was determined to follow its' guidance. "OK." She replied out loud to the thoughts in her head. She returned the photo to its place on the nightstand next to the bed. She didn't want to look at him, so she turned it upside down and laid it on the nightstand next to the bed.

"Merry Christmas! Have you rested enough?" She heard Felipe's voice ask from the other side of the door. "What are you doing in there? Communing with The Morrighan?"

"Very funny!" Morgan yelled. "I'll be dressed in a minute." Morgan said as she put on the clothes that had been laid out for her on the nearby chair. The waiting clothes made it obvious that someone was coming in and out of her room while she was asleep. "Oh well," she thought as she dressed in the quaint, short sleeved, blouse with big embroidered flowers and jeans that had been left for her. Her other clothes had been removed.

When Morgan opened the door, she found Felipe standing there with a bouquet of red roses. "Feliz Navidad, Merry Christmas," he said as he handed them to her.

"Could this guy get any more charming" she thought to herself as she took the roses and put them in the sink that she quickly filled with water.

"There is a vase under the sink," Felipe said as he watched her scurry about looking for a proper container to house the blooms.

"These are lovely," she said and smiled at Felipe. As she put the flowers in the vase, she had a thought. "Aren't roses scarce this time of the year?"

"Yes, they do not grow here in the winter. These came from Mexico City. I got you the red roses because they are symbolic of the Holy Mother, the Virgin of Guadalupe. She is the patroness of Mexico's struggle for Independence. Do you know the story?" he asked as he motioned her to go through the open door and on to the porch.

"No," Morgan said and shook her head accordingly.

"I will tell you some other time. Now we are going to the Christmas dinner that Concha has prepared upstairs. Concha has a big Christmas feast at her house for the relatives of her boy toys. She likes parties. She is very happy that you are feeling well."

"I bet. She can't wait for her brother to suck on me until I'm a raisin," she said and smiled to Felipe as she walked past him and went out the door. He only chuckled and shook his head as he closed the door behind her. He pointed to the nearby stair way and indicated that they had to go up the stairs.

"Have you ever been to a Mexican Christmas dinner?

"No"

"You are really going to enjoy it!" he said as they entered Concha's living room. It also had a wall of glass windows that faced the ocean. The furnishings were the same rattan and wicker that were also in Morgan's room. The furniture was modern and expensive. Many photographs of Mayan ruins adorned the walls. Priceless Mayan statues and other artifacts also decorated the house. The home was filled with people, food and several piñatas hanging from the ceiling. Morgan clung to Felipe. She grabbed his hand as they walked through the room. He chuckled to himself. "Now she is so timid. How fascinating!" he thought and drew her to his side in a sweeping, seemingly romantic gesture. Concha noticed this display of affection and smiled broadly. Felipe was very social as he nodded and mumbled a few words to all the people that they passed as he moved Morgan through the living room. People of all ages were in attendance. Against the far wall was a table of alcohol, ice and mixers. Then, there was the table with the food. It had Mexican tamales in the center. There were five different types of tamales. There was also a platter of sweets at the end of the table.

After Morgan and Felipe filled their plates, Felipe gestured to Morgan to take a seat at the long table that was in the middle of the large living room. When all the guests had found a seat at the table, Concha, is broken Spanish, gave a toast. Everyone raised their glasses. "To a year filled with prosperity and good health," she said and looked right at Morgan.

Morgan was taken aback by the intensity of her stare. Morgan suddenly realized that this was a very important toast to Concha. She wanted all to go as planned with Morgan. While she was giving the toast, Concha recognized that her entire future, her life and all that she had acquired could be gone. In less than three months her brother would come through the dark portal at Boca Negra. Concha realized at that moment that March 21st was the day when all of their fates would collide. Concha thought about Enrique and Eduardo as she sat down. They were on either side of her. "They have it good here," she thought. "I ask so little of them, except when it comes to lovemaking. Then they have to perform according to my demands. I am very demanding," Concha thought as she chuckled at her private joke and smiled at her lovers.

Morgan was finally having a good time. She was enjoying the festive atmosphere, the food and most of all, being around Felipe. She tried not to look at Concha. She did not want to think of what was to come. She just wanted to drink beer and flirt with the sensitive, yet sensual healer. "He is a lovely man. Being with him is like a salve that takes the sting out of this situation. I am happy to have someone who I can admire and look up to here. I feel his heart is pure," Morgan deliberated and smiled warmly at Felipe.

Let The Game Begin

Morgan tried to turn over and open her eyes, but her head hurt. "Too much beer." That was what came into her mind as she was trying to get herself out of bed and into the shower. "Too much beer and not enough sex," she giggled as she thought of the debonair Felipe. She went to the bathroom and started the shower. When the water was at a comfortable temperature, she walked into the middle of the stream and felt a great sense of relief. While the clear, warm fluid passed over her, she kept thinking of what it would be like to have Felipe in there with her.

Shortly after those thoughts crossed her mind, she heard a knock at the door. Felipe's voice was coming from the other side of the door. "OMG, is he reading my mind?" she asked herself as she hurriedly dressed.

"Time for your first lesson," he yelled through the door.

"How did you know that I was up?" she asked out of curiosity and embarrassment as she put on the clothes that were on the chair.

"I could tell you that I tuned into your energy field. But that is not what happened. When you turned on the water, Concha called me to come over," the shaman stated with quiet laughter.

In a few moments Morgan replied with "Come in."

Felipe smiled as he walked into the room and handed her a paper cup of hot coffee.

When Morgan took off the lid and looked at the mocha colored liquid, she broke out into a big smile. "You must be psychic, you knew I liked cream. How did you know that I wanted cream in my coffee?"

"Cream, no sugar. It just seemed right," he grinned and looked away.

"Anyone who does the kind of work that he does must be intuitive," Morgan thought to herself as she took a sip of the hot liquid. "If he can tell what I am feeling, why doesn't he respond?" Morgan was more concerned about Felipe's thoughts of her then what life had in store this morning.

"Come on, we will first go to the house of Lupe. She is the herbalist. She is making the mushroom potion that will take us to the Underworld. She is not quite done with the new batch, so I thought we could go over there and you could meet her.

"OK." Morgan replied as she took another sip of her warm coffee.

"You will like Lupe. She is about your age. I think that you two will bond nicely."

"Is that important to this process?" Morgan asked.

"I don't know. Only Lupe will know that. She is a very sought - after healer. She is extremely skilled at making healing potions and poultices for the sick. Of course Concha uses her to make the potions for the women to take when they are destined to kiss the magician."

"How can she do that?" Morgan said with the familiar irritation coming through her voice.

"If she doesn't, someone else will. Concha pays well. Lupe is really the best in this area. It is good to have the best person make your potions, no?" Felipe shot her a sideways smile. "Don't be afraid of Lupe. She is on our side.'"

"Our side?" Morgan questioned.

"Yes. We are all here to help you. She would like this to end as much as you and I. The only way that will happen is for you to slay Ixma in the Underworld."

"I did some magic mushrooms in high school." Morgan replied sheepishly.

"This will be different. You will only get enough of the potion to allow you to enter the Underworld and to learn how to work with your mind as well as your body. The Underworld is really a realm that is controlled by thought energy. When your subconscious connects with the plant, and you are standing in the portal, you are transported to the Underworld's unique frequency. The mushrooms that you took as a teen were different. Lupe has to make a combination of herbs along with the mushrooms to transport you to the Underworld. When it is not the Solstice or Equinox, you must stand in either a portal or on the quatrefoil at the handball court at a Mayan ruin to go back and forth between these worlds. The quatrefoil looks like an equilateral cross. This is an ancient method of travel that was developed by the tribes before the Maya: The Toltec and the Aztec. The Aztec perfected the ways to use the potion. That is one of the reasons that they are known for their brutality. The potion was given to the sacrificial victims. The warriors captured from battles with other tribes would await their demise without restraints or trauma. The Aztecs performed more human sacrifices then the Maya. "

"Wow," was all Morgan could say. It was a wow that was filled with dread more than shock.

"Don't be afraid, Morgan. You will have just the right amount to be able to be in the Underworld, but to be clear headed and focus. The potion will not affect you as it did before. Everything is carefully mastered. Lupe is an expert at this type of work"

"When do I get to meet the magic cook?" Morgan said as she put down her empty coffee cup.

"We are going to her house right now. Don't forget your hat." Morgan grabbed it as she left the bedroom. When they got to the front of the house, Felipe pointed in the direction of his old truck. It was a weathered Ford that looked like it had put in many years of service. He opened the creaking door for her, smiled, and loudly slammed it shut once she had been seated. After bumping around on the dirt roads of

Playa Del Carmen, Felipe stopped in front of a walled compound that had a yellow door. When they got out, Felipe led Morgan up to the lemon colored entrance. He knocked and then it opened a crack. It was Lupe who opened the door.

"I glad you here. I worried," Lupe stated in broken English. She pulled Morgan into the house by the hand and led her into one of the small rooms off the main courtyard. Felipe followed closely behind her. Once inside, Morgan saw that she was in the laboratory of a master botanist. There were drying plants hanging from the ceiling and along all the walls in the indigenous chemistry lab. There was a long narrow table in the center of the room and a sink by the side wall. There were no windows. All the light in the room came from two bare light bulbs that hung from outlets in the middle of the room. "This workroom, "she said." I mix all the plants used by ancient Maya. Knowledge of sacred plants handed down from families of the three Mayan master herbalists who were famous for potions."

Lupe gave Morgan a little tour of her kitchen. "These plants have many uses. Depends on combinations. Sacred mushrooms are put in many healing potions. They are put in potions for healing a broken heart, inflammations and also arthritis.

"I could use a big dose for the broken heart one" Morgan quietly added.

"Didn't you feel good when you about to kiss Ixma?" she asked innocently.

"Yes, I did." Morgan thought to herself. As she allowed herself to recall that night, she remembered that she did feel happy.

"That is beauty of plant medicine" Lupe nodded in agreement. The petite woman was in her late 30's. She was attired in the traditional dress of the Maya. Her clothing consisted of a hand embroidered blouse of different shades of green that was cinched at the waist. What appeared to be a yard of a green striped material secured the blouse and was wrapped snuggly around the waist. The skirt gave Morgan the impression of a floor length pencil skirt. Lupe had lengthy, black hair. It was neatly tied in a long braid that went down to her waist. She had ribbons that matched the color of her blouse braided in her hair. She gave Morgan a big smile that resembled Felipe's lovely grin. "Relax and allow yourself to open to changes that will come," she said, "It be easier for you"

"And how do I do that?" Morgan asked sincerely.

"Listen to your grandmother. She will guide you in your dreams." Lupe stated in a matter of fact tone.

Morgan was now in a state of disbelief. 'How do you know about my grandmother?" Morgan asked with a serious tone in her voice.

"Your grandmother came to me in a dream. She powerful. How you say Adivino?" said Lupe and looked to Felipe.

"Magician," Felipe said to help Lupe. "Lupe said that your grandmother came to her in a dream and showed her who you are. Your grandmother said you were very devoted to the goddess of Ireland. During the dream, your grandmother told Lupe the name of the goddess you serve, The...

"Morrighan" Morgan stated as she finished Felipe's sentence. "Yes, I have met her, alright."

"The Morrighan has called upon you to heal a tremendous injustice that keeps happening in this world right now. Ixma is negatively impacting the planet with his actions. He is tampering with the balance of dark and light. The Morrighan cannot deal with this situation directly. She needs you. We all need you, Morgan." Felipe's words were laden with emotion.

"I am sorry, but so much has been heaped upon me in the last few days." Morgan said softly and lowered her head. "I can't help but be anxious about this situation. I think I will feel better if I know precisely what I have to do. I want to understand what is expected of me. What are the pitfalls that I should watch out for?"

"You are a fighter! You are already looking for the winning strategy," Felipe thought to himself as he looked into Morgan's eyes.

"We get to that." Lupe said. "First you must learn to move in the Underworld. When you there, it like swimming through a thick soup."

"Well, I like water." Morgan said shyly, feeling The Morrighan's eyes upon her.

"We will see how much you like it," said Lupe, and she handed Morgan a cup of a thick looking liquid.

"Is this the stuff I had when I met the man who could have gotten the super stud award? He is really a midget?" Morgan asked with the familiar tone of disbelief in her voice. She was stuck on that issue: that a gorgeous man could in reality be a repulsive dwarf.

"Ixma's talents of deception are many." Felipe laughed.

Lupe laughed politely too. Morgan smiled and just held the cup of who-knows-what in her hands. "I don't want to drink this until I absolutely have to," Morgan thought.

Then Lupe gave a cup to Felipe. "You must take this to Boca Negra. You won't have to drink any until you get there. We can only enter the Underworld from there," he stated.

Felipe kissed Lupe on the cheek and then turned to leave. His quick nod of the head in Morgan's direction made I clear to her that it was time to go back to the truck. With drinks in hand, Felipe opened the yellow door for Morgan and motioned for her to get inside the vehicle. He gave Morgan his cup once she was situated in the cab. "Hold on to these until we

138

get there. Don't spill any." He said and gave her the look of a father talking to a petulant child.

"Si,si, Senor" she said in a playful tone of voice. It took about 20 minutes for the two to go from Lupe's house to the inlet of Boca Negra. Once they had parked in front of the little buildings, Felipe gestured for his cup. When his was in his hand, he looked at Morgan. With his free hand he made the International signal of "bottoms up." As he put the handmade pottery cup to his lips, he looked sideways to see if Morgan was drinking hers. She was not.

"Now Morgan, don't hesitate. You will be safe. And I will not try to seduce you," he added with a laugh as he exited the vehicle.

"Oh darn!" Morgan said with a laughing tone in her voice as she winked at him and then started to drink the mixture. She downed the thick, soupy drink in two gulps. After the last of it had passed her lips, Morgan sank back into the truck seat. Felipe was now standing by her closed door.

"Oh, no you don't. You need to get out of the truck," Felipe stated. She quickly exited the vehicle. As soon as she was standing next to him, Felipe put his hand in hers. He quickly pulled her over to the out cropping of rocks that had hidden the Mayan dancer just a few nights before. Felipe hurriedly pushed Morgan into the circle of boulders that could not be seen from the fire pit. It was the same ring of stone that had transported her to the Mayan ruins of Uxmal on the Winter Solstice. Morgan could now see that the rocks had Mayan symbols carved upon them. Felipe hastily joined her in the circle.

Then it started. Morgan began to feel herself and her everyday consciousness slipping away. She could hear the same screeching sounds and felt the extreme pressure on her body. It was impossible to tell how long it took for them to be deposited in the handball court of Uxmal, but that is where they ended up. It was daylight. They were hovering above the cross that acted as a portal to the Underworld. Felipe took her hand and they drifted away from the portal to the center of the court. Then he let go of her hand. Morgan saw a group of tourists standing in front of her, looking at the ruins of Uxmal. Next she had the most amazing of feelings as a few Chinese women walked right through her. It felt like her body was made of bubbles that expanded to let the tourists pass and then came back together when the tourists had departed.

Felipe saw what happened to Morgan and mentally remarked; "You just had one of the interesting experiences of being in the Underworld. You can feel people from the other dimensions of the earth plane go through you when you are in the Underworld. Now I want to teach you the secret of moving through the Underworld," the delightful man stated in his mind as he floated toward her. When he was hovering in front of her, he started to talk to Morgan mentally. "You must use your mind as well as your body. The whole trick to gliding through the Underworld is to focus your mind on where you want to go, and then your body will follow. Now watch me," he said. Felipe drifted to the other side of the rectangular, walled area and stopped at the wall.

"I want you to project the idea from your mind that you are coming toward me. That is all that you have to do. Now come to me," Felipe instructed politely.

"OK," Morgan thought. She casually looked at the wall, thought to herself that she wanted to go over there, and did not move an inch.

"I am trying, Felipe!" she stated as her mind filled with frustration.

"Keep trying" he thought back. However, after three more attempts to move, she was still hovering in the same spot.

"I must not be explaining myself correctly." Felipe stated after watching her make another vain attempt to move in the watery Underworld. "Don't just look at the wall. See yourself going to the wall. Project an image in your mind of yourself moving to the other side of the court."

Morgan took a few deep breaths to relieve her frustration, and then closed her eyes. Without much effort, she could see herself, in her mind, going over to the other end of the wall. After what seemed like forever, she felt her body moving. As if she was standing on a flying carpet out of the stories of

Arabian Nights, Morgan moved to the other side of the handball court.

"Wow that was really cool. Instant teleportation, like in Star Trek!" Morgan thought and squealed with glee at her success.

"Yessssss! Gracias a Diosa!!" Felipe thought as he laughed. "You have it!" The sound of his thoughts floated out into the liquid air. "That is the basic idea. Project yourself to a place. Perceive yourself there, and you will be there. Soon it will become second nature to you. You will be able to do it without as much mental effort," he suggested. Morgan looked up at the sky. Even though she did not realize that she thought about moving her body up in the air, she suddenly found herself surging quickly up into the sky.

Morgan thought this was fun at first. When she was about 500 feet above the ground, and did not feel herself slowing down, she felt herself panic. She started to scream mentally, "Help; I want to go back down NOW" and she saw herself proceeding downward toward the handball court. Instantly she was plummeting down to the ground.

Before she hit the surface, Felipe scooped her up in his arms. He stopped her descent. "You need to be careful to watch your emotions in the Underworld. It all gets amplified. You can use your emotions to intensify your movement. They can be used to move faster or slower, depending upon what you are feeling. I see you have already experienced that!" He laughed to try to lighten Morgan's mood.

"You would have plunged down into the earth and probably been stuck there if I had not stopped you," Felipe added with an admonishing tone. Even though they were floating in the Underworld, Morgan was enjoying the feeling of being cradled in Felipe's arms. Morgan couldn't believe how good it felt to be in a man's arms.

"Touch is really amplified in the Underworld," he said as he gently released her. It was his way of being polite. He had felt her thoughts.

"Do you see yourself going first and then the rest of you goes?" Morgan said, focusing back on her fascination with this new way to move.

"That is a very good way to put it. What happens is that your soul body goes first, and then the physical body follows. The psyche is stronger than the physical body in the Underworld. I could not give you this explanation until you actually did it. It would have no meaning before you had the experience. Even my words are not really adequate in describing this form of movement." Felipe smiled as he floated away from her. He stopped at the opposite end of the handball court.

"Now come to me." He stated to Morgan. She closed her eyes, pictured herself hovering next to him, opened her eyes, and saw herself moving. She stopped a few feet away from him. While she was floating toward Felipe, she remembered her first night in the Underworld. She decided, as she got closer to Felipe, to go beyond her embarrassment and share with him what happened.

"The night of the Solstice, when we were up on the pyramid, I started being playful with the dancer. I moved away from him, and then he followed me." Morgan thought and lowered her head to avoid Felipe's eyes. "I kept moving away from the Mayan dancer. I enjoyed teasing him. I see now that my feelings of what I wanted to do, of the way I wanted to move, allowed me to go. At first, I just floated up the pyramid like I was in an elevator."

"That was Ixma, using his mind, to bring you to where he wanted you." Felipe said. He realized that she instinctively knew how to move, even though she had never learned.

"You are doing better than I thought for your first time," Felipe thought. "We will be practicing this for the next month. Then, when you have learned how to maneuver swiftly in the Underworld, you will understand the way to play the handball game. "

"I can see that there are many aspects to keep in mind in order to navigate in the Underworld." Morgan thought to herself pensively. "This is a bit tricky, but I know I can do it"

"Sure you can!" Felipe thought emphatically. "Another person's mind is easy to read in the Underworld. If I spoke to you in Spanish, you would

144

not hear me, because the language does not compute in your mind. You would get a feeling, a sense of what I am thinking, but not a verbal message. You seem to be a quick learner. How are you feeling?"

Morgan thought for a moment and then realized that she was suddenly feeling very tired. "A bit worn out," she stated honestly.

"That is ok for today. You have had enough. Now I will show you how we can exit the Underworld before the drug wears off. Let's go back to the cross. We must always come and go through the portal that the cross creates. It is the bridge to both worlds. When the potion is still active in your system and you hover in the cross for a few moments, it will start the process of taking you back through the portal to Boca Negra." Felipe gestured for Morgan to join him in the quatrefoil. Once she was hovering inside the cross, she experienced the same feelings of pressure and noise that went along with transportation to and from the Underworld. Everything went white, and she heard the screeching sound and felt the pressure. She found herself back in the stone circle at Boca Negra. Morgan sunk to the ground. "I feel like I weigh 300 pounds" she thought as she tried to get up. Exhaustion had overtaken Morgan. Felipe came through the portal right behind her and stood next to her.

"At this point in your development, it would not be wise to stay there long. It is not good to run out of energy in the Underworld. Then it is hard to direct yourself. That is why you must build up your stamina and familiarity with the Underworld." When Felipe was done with the lecture, he stretched out his hand to her. She grasped it and in an instant she was standing erect. Then Felipe pulled Morgan out of the stone ring.

"Thanks. I can see that I will have no desire to go to Disneyland when I get back to the states. This is definitely an E ticket ride. "

"E ticket?' Felipe said.

She just waved her hand in a gesture of "never mind" and shook her head as she laughed. Morgan was impressed with this experience. For some reason, a feeling of immense elation came over her. She had succeeded at something. She hadn't known that feeling for a long time. She had mastered Yoga, horseback riding and Qi Gong, but this was something completely different.

"You are feeling good, no?" Felipe asked as he came up behind her.

"Very good," Morgan replied. She was in a positive frame of mind. Then she turned her attention to what had just occurred in the Underworld. She was fascinated that he could sense what she was thinking.

"You are feeling good because that is s symptom of leaving the Underworld before the drug wears off. You are able to return with the ecstasy that the drug gives you when you come back. You will be feeling a bit of it for the next few hours. It will wear off by nightfall"

"I am ok if it doesn't wear off. " Morgan laughed. She did feel light and cheerful.

Felipe now seemed serious. "The mushroom drink is not a replacement for a few beers. It is a sacred herb that is used for ceremonial purposes only. It is not for recreational purposes." He said as he walked away. He appeared to be in a huff.

Morgan followed him and tried to apologize. "I didn't mean to sound like a drug addict. I am just happy to be out of my depression." Morgan stated. She was really trying to back pedal quickly. She did not want to offend Felipe.

"No, but you must not think of the drug as a joy ride. You have too much to learn in a very short a time."

Morgan got up and walked toward him. "I didn't mean to offend you. I'm sorry."

"I know that you did not mean any harm. Americans always think of everything in terms of pleasure seeking. Our plant medicines have been abused by your people for many years." He stopped his tirade and then became quiet. "Please forgive me, Morgan. I am a very serious man. I have a bit of an Irish temper too. You will find out much about me as our lessons continue." He said. They made the return trip to Morgan's abode in silence. She kept reliving the day's events in her mind. A smile emerged on her face as she affirmed within herself that she was successful at something new today. She was happy to be with Felipe, but she was also pleased to be engaged in some activity that challenged her. She became aware that she liked to dig within herself to go beyond a dilemma and overcome it. It was the first time she had felt useful or successful in many years.

"I guess I am getting in touch with my inner warrior," Morgan thought to herself as Concha's home came into view.

A Visit To Ix Chel

Felipe and Morgan had been practicing movement in the Underworld with the sacred medicine for almost a month. Morgan was beginning to enjoy their workouts in the Underworld. She felt like she was learning a new sport, like Karate. When Felipe came to pick her up at her door, he announced that there was an adjustment in their daily schedule.

"We are doing something different today. Or should I say that you are going to have a break from our practice routine this morning. You are going on a little trip to Cozumel with Lupe. It is the day on the sacred Mayan calendar, the Tzolkin, when it is good to give offerings to a deity. You must make an offering to IX Chel, the Mayan goddess of the moon, fertility and childbirth. The place where you landed on shore was directly across from the remains of her temple. You must give thanks for the help that she gave you. Lupe will answer any questions that you have on your way to the island." Felipe announced.

Morgan was a bit let down. She so enjoyed zooming around the Underworld with Felipe. She was beginning to see that she has feelings for him. They had so much fun chasing each other around in the Underworld. She loved to make him smile and laugh. She did not want to appear petulant, so she hid her disappointment. She did as she was requested and followed Felipe as he walked to his waiting truck that had the motor running. Lupe was inside. She had a large basket on her lap. She gave Morgan a big smile when she saw her.

"We going to do fire ceremony at ruins of the main temple to Ix Chel, moon goddess of Maya." Lupe announced. She was also very formal. Morgan was beginning to see that was their way. They cruised slowly toward the harbor in Felipe's truck. When they got to the ferry, about a half-hour later, they found out there was one going to Cozumel in ten minutes.

"You two are going to have a wonderful day. It will be good for you to pay homage to Ix Chel. She did save you, you know." Felipe said. You washed up very close to remains of what was a great shrine to Ix Chel. In the time of the ancient Maya, many people came to pay homage to her. She had a big, beautiful temple. Now all that remains of her place of worship are a Mayan arch and a circular stone where the offerings were put."

"We lucky that we can make use of same stone as my ancestors to pay homage." Lupe stated.

Morgan tried to be respectful as they boarded the ferry to Cozumel. Once they were seated, Morgan started to question Lupe about the Mayan moon goddess. "I don't know anything about Ix Chel. I'd like to know whatever you can tell me about her before we do the ceremony. I have a goddess connection too." Morgan stated sheepishly.

"The Morrighan. She very forceful. Ix Chel nothing like her. She is gentle and loving." Lupe explained. "We do have goddesses in Maya tradition that are fierce. Ix Chel is very gentle and loving. She is mother we all wanted to have growing up" Lupe stated. "Let's sit in quiet during the boat ride." Lupe said. "Allow yourself to be open to Ix Chel. She may come to you while we are on boat."

"OK" Morgan thought. "I will be quiet" Besides; the thought made Morgan think about her own mother.

While they were sitting on the ferry, being propelled to the island of Cozumel, Morgan was lulled into a light trance. Shortly after she sat back on the hard metal benches and closed her eyes, she was soon resting in a lovely forest. It was daytime, and the birds were singing and the butterflies fluttering. Then, at the edge of the clearing, Morgan saw her mother. She ran to her mother and gave her a big embrace. "Mom, I am so glad that you are here! Where have you been?"

"It was the wish of The Morrighan that I disconnect from you. Have you met her?"

Morgan could be seen chuckling with closed eyes. "Oh, yeah, I have encountered her."

As only a mother can do, her mother read Morgan's response easily. "Don't be sarcastic, little one. I had to leave the day you married. It was the will of The Morrighan. She did not want me to help you."

"Help me with what?" Morgan asked in her mind.

"Have a child. I had you, and that saved me from her service. I could not interfere. The Morrighan can have all who pledged themselves to her in a past life called into service in their present life. A priestess can avoid service if she has a female child before the age of thirty. Then the new child becomes dedicated to The Morrrighan. It is a timeless custom, but in many ways just. It is a great honor to be in service to The Morrighan. She will send you on missions that serve the planet and some that just serve her. You may be of service in many ways, not just as a warrior."

Morgan thought to ask, "What do you mean, ma?" Her mother did not respond to her question. She began to disappear.

"MOMMMM" Morgan cried aloud. This shook her out of the altered state. It also made her sad. She opened her eyes and looked out at the ocean as the boat cut through the grayish blue water. "Mom" Morgan thought. "Mom, when are you coming back into my life?" Morgan said as she closed her eyes again and sobbed on and off through the rest of the trip to the island.

As the engine of the boat changed gears and they started to come into the docks, Morgan sat up abruptly. Lupe put her hand on Morgan's arm and smiled. "You had a good rest. You will be ready for the walk. Cozumel is very flat. It is an island. It is an easy walk from the bus stop."

"Bus stop?" Morgan asked.

"Yes. We take bus when we get off the ferry. It will take us to ruin. Then we do ceremony" Lupe smiled as she talked to Morgan.

"Sounds good." Morgan said.   "Ceremony?" Morgan echoed in her mind. "I hope I don't have to be naked in public." When she had this thought, she flashed back to her coming of age ceremony on the cold Santa Monica beach. She started giggling. Lupe noticed her laughter and the two smiled at each other.

They went from the ferry to the bus quickly. In about 20 minutes, after several stops, Lupe got up from her bus seat. Morgan took this as her cue to arise as well. "We get off now," Lupe said as she gathered her big basket off the seat. The breaks on the bus let out a horrifying squeal as it came to a stop. The two women got off quickly. Morgan followed Lupe. Morgan could see that Lupe was heading toward a large, open grass covered area that she assumed to be ruins. It had been cleared away, so that the few remaining stones from the once majestic structure could be seen. Morgan did not know what she was doing, where she was going or what would happen. Everything had been so extraordinary so far; she did not know what to expect. For the first time, Morgan actually felt she could relax and just trust that all was OK. She knew that she had nothing to fear. She felt that she was safe and cared for. Maybe Ix Chel was speaking to her. Morgan was thankful to see her mother again, even if only in a vision. A smile came over her face as she walked with Lupe.

"We here," said Lupe as they approached a pointed Mayan arch. It was standing alone in the middle of what must have been an open courtyard. There were many large stones scattered about. When Morgan got to the arch, she had the feeling that she wanted to kneel. She did not feel embarrassed by the other tourists walking around.

"Pull the hood of your sweat shirt over your head." Lupe said as she noticed that there were a lot of people milling around. "We will be attracting attention, so keep covering on and head down."

"Alright." Morgan nodded in agreement. She wanted to watch what Lupe was doing.

Lupe took her basket to the stone in the middle of the open area. She was kneeling on the ground and was pulling many things out of her basket. Morgan acted on her urge to kneel and did so next to Lupe. She saw a bag of sugar; candles, little round balls, flowers, a bottle of rum and more come out of Lupe's basket. "Do you want to know what all of these items for?" Lupe asked as she started to set up the ceremonial fire.

"Sure" Morgan said. She realized that she did sincerely wanted to know more about the Mayan culture.

First Lupe picked the bag of sugar. After she opened one end, she started to pour out the sugar to form a circle about two feet in diameter. "First we put circle. This represents world. Then we cut it into four sections. This represents four directions: North, South, East and West." Then Lupe put a dot into each of four sections. "Now circle is same as Mayan glyph Quiniel. This is Mayan astrology sign that is called in English: Star. The day sign Quiniel is very sacred to Maya. It stands for death and rebirth. It also represents the planet Venus. This planet goes away in sky and then returns. The story of Kukhulkan is same. It is story of death and rebirth"

"Why does it represent death and rebirth?" Morgan asked.

"Old story, but I tell you" Lupe said. "The old Mayan king, Kukhulkan, was bad king. He make many mistakes. Worst was sex with sister" Lupe said in a matter-of-fact tone.

Morgan let out a loud sigh as she sucked in air in disbelief. "A king slept with his sister???""

Lupe laughed, "King felt bad. Wanted to kill self. He sailed away in a boat on fire. In few months he returned. He changed man. He good man. He make good leader to people."

"That sounds like a happy story." Morgan added with a smile.

"It is. He then be good ruler to people. We use the day sign Quiniel to remind us that we can all change and be our better self."

Those words hit home to Morgan and she withdrew into silence. In an instant, Morgan realized that she was going through a transition as well. These changes, which had been thrust upon her, were bringing out hidden aspects that were latent within her. It suddenly became clear to Morgan that the life she had lived, that had only used a fraction of her potential, had to be taken away. Morgan sensed that a new existence, a different type of life, was waiting for her. The abrupt transformations that she had recently experienced would put her in touch with her new life. Then, she had a knowing, deep within her. She felt sure that a new path would present itself at the right time. The power that this ancient ritual was starting to manifest was beginning to affect her. It gave her the awareness that she would make it through this challenge to her new life. Maybe Ix Chel was talking to her?

"Now we put the candles. They also stand for the four directions. That is why they four different colors: red for east, blue for west, white for north and yellow for south. They represent all earth, all peoples." Lupe arranged the candles in a circular fashion within her creation. They were all tied together. Lupe fanned them out evenly in the circle. "Now we put chips of Copal. It is offering to gods. Next I put rum. This will also make fire burn strong." By the time that Lupe was done, Morgan saw before her a pyramid-shaped formation. The candles had been arranged in such a way as to stand up over the other ingredients that had been piled up underneath. Lupe stood up for a moment to look at it and then fell to her knees in prayer, in a language that Morgan did not understand.

Morgan did not know what was happening, but she knew by now to do as Lupe did. She also bent her head. In about five minutes, Lupe got to her feet, sprinkled more rum on the offering and started to light the fire. As soon as she put the Bic to it, it went up in a substantial blaze. Then Lupe came back to kneel alongside of Morgan. While a whole group of spell bound tourists looked on, Lupe seemed unconcerned. She appeared to be lost in trance. She kept muttering unspoken words and moved her torso back and forth. Morgan remained silent, her head bent in reverence while the fire burned.

In about a half hour, the fire had died down. Lupe ended their silence and spoke to Morgan. "The ceremony done in Nahuatl. That is Mayan language that honors Ix Chel." Lupe explained. "I ask goddess for your safety. You need protection. You landed here. She kept you alive. She must have smiled on you. She know that you have great mission to do. Lupe looked at her and grinned. "She wants you to succeed. Many children have not been able to come into the world because women killed. Ixma very bad man." Lupe said and shiver went down her back. "I know that you can destroy him." Lupe said

Morgan felt overwhelmed. "I have never killed anyone before," Morgan said with emphasis.

Lupe laughed at this sentence. "Do not think of him as a person. He is evil demon. You been chosen to stop Ixma. It is time. You will get what you need to do it. Ix Chel told me when I prayed. Now we go." Lupe had to stay focused on the task at hand: getting out of this place without being noticed.

Indeed, there was a big crowd standing around the fire. A tour guide came up to them, saw Lupe dressed in her traditional garb, and then walked away. Morgan definitely heard the tour guide say "Damn Mayans" under her breath.

Lupe waited a few minutes and then started to walk away as the remnants of the fire still lingered. "Don't you want to put some water on the fire?" Morgan asked, her Girl Scout training kicking in.

"It be very bad luck to put out fire. Gods would be angry. Ix Chel might send problems to us. It will be ok." Lupe assured her.

Morgan's eyes opened wide. "I don't want to upset any gods, goddesses. I want them all to be happy. " Morgan said as she fell in line behind Lupe. As they walked away, Morgan heard the hissing sound of water being poured on the fire. Lupe turned around quickly to catch the tour guide walking away from the dead embers carrying a bucket.

"Bad luck for her!" Lupe stated simply and continued to walk back to the bus stop.

"How did you come to learn about plants and healing herbs?" Morgan asked as they settled down in the bus for the short ride back to the ferry.

"After I went through Shaman's Death, my grandmother taught me. She descended from Mayan priestess at Tulum. She was dedicated to Ix Chel and lived her life as her priestess. She had many children for Ix Chel"

Morgan thought about this. She wondered if Lupe meant what she thought she meant: that her ancestor had a lot of intercourse with men who were not their husbands.

"In old times priestess had a lot of sex" Lupe replied, answering Morgan's unasked question.

"She has got to be reading my mind" Morgan thought as she listened.

"In those times, woman dedicated to the goddess never had own family. She be with many men on feast days. That way, no one knows who is father. That way, child belongs to Ix Chel."

"Oh," was all that Morgan could say. Somehow that whole scenario seemed very familiar to Morgan. On the way home, Morgan started to wonder if she had done that for The Morrighan in her past lives.

When they got on the ferry that was to take them back to Playa Del Carmen, Lupe gave further suggestions to Morgan. "Close eyes and see if Ix Chel has message for you," Lupe said. She sat back, put her brightly colored Mayan shawl over her head and became silent.

Morgan did as directed and sank into a trance easily. It only took a few minutes for her to start to see a scene. Suddenly, she saw the temple to Ix Chel, as it had been during the peak of the Mayan empire. She started to walk through the rooms of the temple. She then began to see the priestesses of Ix Chel. They were lovely, young women with long black hair, wearing loose robes of pink and green. They seemed to be preparing for some type of celebration. Morgan felt it was a feast day. Women were carrying baskets of food, and other items. The offerings were laid out on a cloth decorated with vibrant patterns. It was positioned in front of the place of worship. Then what Morgan saw next took her breath away: she saw herself, dressed as a priestess of Ix Chel. Morgan saw herself arranging the table of food. She could see the faces of the other women. They seemed familiar, somehow.

In a few moments, another woman came out of the temple. All the priestesses turned and bowed to the woman who obviously represented the goddess Ix Chel. Suddenly, Morgan heard music. Then people gathered, all dressed in clothing that must have been worn during the time of the ancient Maya. People came from all directions. They brought baskets of food and clay pitchers of drink. The jugs were set next to the food. All the people were filing by a small, solitary cloth. It was covered with flowers. In the middle of the tapestry sat a clay bowel, decorated with Mayan glyphs. Once in front of the cloth, a priestess would hand each person a drinking cup that held the contents of the basin. One at a time, they quickly ingested the contents of the mug and then handed it back to the priestess. When all the participants had gone before the ceremonial bowl and all had a drink, the feasting and the music started.

After talking briefly, the people started to dance. It was not like our dancing of today. It was dancing in a line. The men and women formed two separate lines and then created their own circles. The male ring was on the outside. It was going in a clockwise direction. The woman's was on the inside. They were going counter clockwise. One by one, the men and women split off from the circles and paired up. Then the priestesses were left. The men left behind then formed a circle around the women. The two small circles started to move to a slow, hypnotic rhythm.

Morgan could feel the energy of these two circles as she watched them in her vision. As the men and women swayed to the music in their circles, a thin white haze started to settle upon the dancers in the two circles. Somehow Morgan knew that this shimmering mist was the essence of IX Chel. The vapor was descending upon the soon- to- be- lovers. In short order, the opalescent fog was covering all the people in the two circles. The music suddenly stopped, and the men and women stopped moving and faced each other. What Morgan saw next was astounding. She recognized the face of Felipe on the man that was standing before her. Felipe grabbed her and then they sank down on the ground. Suddenly, the vision faded.

When Morgan opened her eyes, the ferry was floating into the port. As the boat came to a stop, Morgan composed herself. She was a bit shaken by the vision. "Felipe?" she thought. It was more than Morgan could take. She started to cry. Everything has been so odd lately. As she got off the ferry, Morgan was working hard to hold back the tears. She silently followed the herbalist to a bench near the ferry dock. Lupe took out her cell phone and made a quick call.

Lupe could see in her face that Morgan was having a hard time. "Let's have lunch while we wait for Felipe," she said in a very kind and tender tone of voice. In Lupe's bottomless enchanted basket, there was also food to eat. Lupe pulled out some sandwiches made of seasoned beef, avocado and salsa on large rolls. She handed one to Morgan. She was still too overwhelmed to eat, but wanted to be courteous. Morgan took the wrapped sandwich and gave Lupe a small smile. Morgan could not bring herself to open it and put it to her lips.

"I know this hard for you" Lupe said.

"I saw Felipe and myself in another time, doing a ceremony." Morgan said

"You saw a past life with Felipe. There is a reason that the goddess of the Irish came to him and to you. You both have a connection that goes back more than this life. We Maya know that we are the latest version

162

of our ancestors." Lupe smiled and then started to open up her meal. Morgan started to cry. In a short time, she got off the bench, in dire need of Kleenex. Morgan saw a little store near the area for boarding the ferry. She went in and the woman just handed her a box. The woman did not ask for money, but just waved her out of the store. Morgan took the box, still sobbing and walked back to the bench where Lupe was drinking a can of juice. Morgan kept sobbing for a few more minutes and then started to calm down. Lupe handed her a container of juice. This time Morgan was able to get some of the liquid into her body. Morgan was beginning to breathe regularly again. She was taking sips of her juice when Lupe started to talk.

"The goddess has given you healing, Morgan. She showed you that you have been here before and what you have done. You now clearing what you went through before you arrived today. She is working with you Morgan. The vision you had, what was it?'

"Felipe and I were doing a ceremony, a dance. Then we faced each other. I guess we were going to have sex, but then the vision faded"

Lupe started to laugh. "You and Felipe? My cousin? That funny."

"Felipe is your cousin?" Morgan said with an undertone of amazement in her voice.

Lupe was full of giggles. "Yes. He lives in the house with us. It is family house. His part of the house is behind the blue door."

"That is nice," was all that Morgan could say at the moment.

"It is very good" Lupe said happily, clapping her hands. "You had a memory! The goddess is pleased with you. You need to know that she has blessed you. She showed you that you have been in her service too. You priestess to many goddesses, no?"

Morgan's response was to start on a new wave of tears.

"Can't go back, Morgan. Can only go forward to new life. That is why you here .Do not worry. The goddess give you vision, she will protect you. She show you that you are one of us. She will save you from harm in Underworld. "

Morgan was beginning to feel better. She liked the protection idea. She liked the idea that she did not have to worry. She felt a lot of loving energy when she thought of the Mayan deity.

"I believe you, Lupe.' Morgan said sincerely through her tears.

Morgan became quiet as her thoughts flew back to the vision of her and the attractive shaman. She came face to face with her feelings for Felipe. Feelings that she wanted to suppress, but could not. He seemed to be sensitive to her, and he seemed to appreciate her. "Is he being nice to me just because it is his job? Does he really care?" Morgan wondered as she continued to weep.

While she was sobbing, Lupe added, "My cousin like you. He think you very smart." Morgan knew that Lupe was trying to be nice, but it just made her cry all the more. "Don't worry. When this all over, you two will be together." Lupe said confidently.

"What makes you say that?" Morgan said, trying to speak through a choked up throat." He is just being nice to me because he has to."

"No" Lupe said strongly. "The goddess show me vision too. I also see picture of ceremony where you first met. Now you be reunited. The goddess show me. Don't worry. "

Morgan shook her head up and down, as if to say ok, yes and thank you. She was already attracting attention to herself. She needed to calm down. She could not risk being found. Each day brought more confirmations to her that she needed to follow through with this trial. Aside from the fact that The Morrighan could destroy her at any minute if she tried to back out of this challenge, she was in love and could not stand being without him. She desperately wanted the glimpse of the past with Felipe to come again in this life. She wished that Felipe would throw her down on the ground and take her, like he was going to do in the vision.

"He seems distant, so reserved. He doesn't like me." Morgan said out loud.

"Yes he does, Morgan. You both have job to do. You are doing good with the trips to the Underworld. Soon you will be able to start learning to play the handball game. Just keep going and you will get through this. Then you be together."

Morgan wanted to believe Lupe. After a few more minutes, Morgan took some long, deep breaths. She was breathing like her yoga instructor had taught her, and she released some of the emotions. In a short time, Morgan actually had a smile on her face. She was coming back to Felipe!

Dumb And Dumber

As the days progressed, Morgan had increased her skill at functioning in the Underworld. Her natural dexterity as an athlete emerged easily. She could now maneuver in the Underworld quite well. She had a lot of fun playing there with Felipe too. Morgan was beginning to feel much better. She did not realize that having people around her who cared was the healing her spirit needed.

Morgan's body had become used to the potion that took her to the Underworld. She grew accustomed to the routine: Potion on an empty stomach, then chasing Felipe around the Underworld or him chasing her. Felipe had told her that she was doing well.

That morning, when Morgan heard the familiar knock on her door, she opened it to an awful surprise. Eduardo and Enrique, Concha's cabana boys, were standing at the door, with a big sack in hand. Morgan began to panic. Then Felipe arrived. Morgan began to breathe easier and relax. She was still on high alert. She needed to find out what was going on.

"Good morning, Morgan. You look radiant today." Felipe said. Morgan gave him a piercing glance. Enrique gave the bag to Felipe.

"Don't try to butter me up" she thought to herself. Then she said aloud "What is going on here, Felipe???"

"Morgan, Enrique and Eduardo have come to help you learn to play the game of handball that the Maya of old played in the Underworld. We will all take the potion. Then these fellows will be there to assist me as I show you how to play the Mayan handball game."

"OK." She said slowly. What else could she say? "I am a prisoner, aren't I?" she thought as the events of the morning showed her the reality of her situation. She followed Felipe to his truck and got in. He threw the gear into the back of the truck, got in and started up the motor. They rambled slowly toward Boca Negra.

"Do they have to come?" Morgan whined as they approached the dark portal.

"It is time Morgan. You have to learn to play the handball game. They need to observe your progress. Did you think this day would not arrive?" he said emphatically.

Morgan sighed and was quiet for a moment before answering. "No. In the back of my mind, I knew it, but facing the reality is hard."

"Yes, I know. Concha wants to see how you are progressing. That is why you must show the boys that you can maneuver in the Underworld. Just because they have to wait until March 21st for this to take place, does not mean they are patient. Do your best and show them that you are progressing with your time there," he added with an upbeat tone in his voice.

Morgan turned away from the man she was now deeply in love with and stared out the window. The cold truth of what she was being called upon to do was starting to become real. "I guess I have to face the fact that I must fight the scuzzy magician. I just need to wrap my head around that," she stated after taking several deep breaths.

Felipe just chuckled as he listened to her cute phrases and her deep breathing. "Everything is charming about her," he thought to himself. He suppressed the warm feeling that was about to engulf him, as he turned his head away from her direction. "I can't let her see how much she as affects me. She must keep her mind on the task ahead of her."

"I know that I have shoved the end result to the back of my mind," she admitted when she saw him finally turn to look at her.

"It is time for those thoughts to move to the front of your mind. You have a great test ahead of you. Now that you have gotten used to the Underworld, it is time to be serious." Felipe said." You must learn how to play the game. You need to be able to move the rubber ball around and get it through your stone circle on the court. That is how the game works. It is a combination of physical and mental prowess. You have the basics of movement down, but you need to learn to play the game and become adept at it."

When they arrived at Boca Negra, Felipe got out of the truck quickly, went to the rear and got the handball gear. Then he went to the front and asked Morgan to get the thermos that held the potions. "Please remember to take the plastic cups that are next to you. I know you are still in a state of shock." They had been brought along to share the contents of the thermos.

He shot Morgan a look that said, "Move it! Let's get going!" Morgan got the message and was out of the truck, with the cups and the thermos in a flash. Morgan and Felipe solemnly walked to the stone circle, hidden by rocks, that was the doorway to the Underworld.

Eduardo and Enrique were there waiting near the stone ring for the pair. They were chatting and laughing quietly. When they saw Morgan, they suddenly became quiet. While the boys watched, Felipe ceremoniously took the ancient handball equipment out of its bag while standing right next to the stone ring.

"Come here, Morgan. I am going to put the handball regalia on you. Then we will drink the potions and go to the Underworld." From the leather bag, Felipe pulled out a long belt. It was braided with leather and twine. There were balls the size of apricots evenly spaced along the belt. It had designs on it that Morgan had come to realize were Mayan glyphs. The girdle had a crotch piece that was attached from the center of the belt in the front and fastened in the back. Felipe politely put the belt

170

around her hips and pulled the connecting leather strap through her legs to her posterior. He fastened it quickly over her loose fitting jeans.

There were also thick leather boots that she had to put on. Morgan realized that the only way the boots would fit is if she wrapped the extra material of her jeans around her calves. Then Felipe helped her into the boots. They were snug but tolerable. Last out of the bag was the leather breast plate. It was a thick, square piece of animal hide that was meant to protect the upper body. At the top of the protective chest gear, anchored at each end, was a leather strap that fit over the head to hold the top of the breastplate in place. There were two leather straps that were attached to the breast plate on each side, half way down. These were to be tied in the middle of the back. "Hold the breastplate next to your body until I secure it, Morgan." Once on, it covered her from her collar bone to the bottom of her ribs. It took Morgan a few moments to get her balance. The weight of the outfit made it difficult to move.

Felipe quickly handed her a cup of the potion. Morgan immediately downed the drink, and Felipe did the same. Felipe picked up the handball bag, took Morgan's hand and they stepped into the stone circle. The pair was instantly transported to Uxmal. The cabana boys took their potions and quickly followed.

When they came through to the handball court of Uxmal, Morgan was delightfully surprised to find that the weight of the regalia would not be a hindrance to movement in the Underworld. Even though the apparatus for the game was very heavy, in the Underworld Morgan could zoom around without a problem. "This outfit is ok. You'd never find it on Rodeo Drive in Beverly Hills!" she joked to herself. Enrique chuckled and looked at her. Morgan remembered that he understood English and could hear her thoughts. Eduardo was smiling, but Morgan realized he had not understood her.

"Morgan," said Enrique, using a sensual tone in his voice. "You look very fine in your handball outfit. Just remember, when you play game with Ixma, this is all that you will have on. It is Mayan tradition to play the game naked except for the ceremonial regalia." He gave her a big Cheshire Cat smile. Enrique laughed and looked to Eduardo for support. They both chuckled and then looked away.

"Here is the ball that we send through the stone rings," Felipe stated. He brought out the rubber ball from the leather bag. It was the size of a grapefruit. It appeared to be very heavy, but floated in the air when he threw it into the court.

"Felipe is acting different," she said to herself. Morgan did not feel the kind, nurturing vibe that she had been enjoying coming from him now. She looked to him for support but did not find any.

Suddenly, Felipe motioned for Morgan to go to the far end of the handball court. She did what he indicated, but had a questioning look in her eyes. Felipe started to talk to her, in a formal tone, using his mind. They all knew that they could read each other's thoughts. Morgan decided that Concha's boys would get no information from her. "I am going to keep my mind on the game," she thought as the men smiled and nodded.

When she had floated to the far end of the court, Felipe mentally told her to turn around. She had gravitated to the end of one wall. "Good, Morgan. You have picked a side. Your goal is to get the ball through the circle on the opposite side. You start from your end of the court. The way the game is played is to use your belt to move the ball around. That is all you can use. No hands, feet."

"OK," She thought.

"Alright, then we are ready to go!" Felipe thought enthusiastically. "One of the boys will serve to you. The ball must dip toward the ground at least once before you approach it. Then you can hit it toward the stone circle with your hip."

Enrique, the brains of Concha's duo, floated to the opposite end of the court and hovered near his stone ring. He had the ball with him. When he got to his side, he tossed the ball into the court area. It floated toward Morgan. She approached it easily. She got close to the ball and then rammed it as hard as she could with her hip. It went a few feet but did not get near the stone circle on Enrique's side of the court.

The ball was now starting to sink towards the ground. "Try again, Morgan" Felipe said softly. "Go after it and hit it toward your goal, Morgan. Hit it with your hip." When she got closer to the ball, she angled her body so that she would be able to whack it with the side of her hip. Her hip made contact with the ball. Instead of moving the ball toward the ring, it went sideways and out of the court. Concha's lovers started laughing. Then Eduardo retrieved the ball and threw it back into the court again.

"Ok Morgan" Felipe said. "I will send the ball to you again. This time don't hit it so hard. A little force goes a long way in the Underworld. Just tap it with your hip and get it in the stone circle."

Morgan did as she was instructed. All accept the part about getting the ball to go through the stone ring. Enrique got the sphere and then repeated the same throw of the ball. The ball started coming slowly toward her. When she got her hip close to the ball, she gave it a tap. The ball started sailing toward the circle but was about five feet off the mark.

More chuckles from Enrique and Eduardo. This made Morgan's face turn red.

"I see that Irish temper coming out" Felipe said as he retrieved the ball and started again.

The next time, when Morgan hit the ball with her hip, it got closer to the ring, but the ball sailed past it.

"I am going to have one of the guys send you the ball. You are doing better. Aim your hip so you can send it near the ring." Enrique sent the ball to her a little faster, and she hit it. It went spinning out of the court.

After the seventh fruitless attempt to get the ball through the ring, Morgan exploded. "Get me out of here!!" were the words that screamed into Felipe and Enrique's minds. Felipe quickly realized that Morgan had reached a breaking point. He instinctively knew that it would be pointless to push her further. Felipe came up behind Morgan and pushed her into the cross at the far end of the court. They were back in the stone ring of Boca Negra in a few moments. As Felipe was helping Morgan off with her boots, Enrique and Eduardo returned. They smiled politely and waved good-by as they sped off in the Mercedes convertible.

Go Into The Trees

The shaman and the priestess rode back to Concha's house in silence. Felipe opened the door for her and stepped back to let her pass. She walked into the room and slammed the door behind her. It startled the guard on the porch. She made it clear that she did not want to talk or hear anything from anyone. Felipe got the message. "I will come by tomorrow. We will practice without the fellows for a while," he said in a soft voice.

She stripped her clothes off and got into the shower. "The water is so comforting and soothing. "Water makes everything better," she thought to herself as she closed her eyes and stood under the shower head. She closed her eyes and let the water run over her whole body. About 10 minutes had passed with Morgan situated under the stream of soothing moisture.

"I am glad that you are enjoying the water. It is what gives us strength." This thought caused Morgan to step out of the spray of the shower and open her eyes. A bright green glow filled the bathroom.

Morgan was afraid to get out of the shower. "Now, my dearest, do not be frightened of me. I am here to help you enjoy yourself. We are going to know incredible pleasure this evening!"

This last bit of information made Morgan really afraid to get out of the shower. "Come, my dear, you must get dressed for this festive night." Morgan grabbed a towel that was hanging on a nearby hook and wrapped it around her. When she got out, she saw what she hoped would not be there: The Morrighan. Morgan didn't realize that she had a great fear of displeasing The Morrighan until now.

"Maybe this is past life conditioning," Morgan told herself as she turned to face the creature that had taken over the bathroom and turned it bright green. She could tell that she was connecting with past-life feelings of being a servant to the green-eyed bombshell. She felt the energy of submission come over her. Strangely, it seemed comfortable. It gave Morgan the notion of safety. Suddenly, Morgan realized that The Morrighan had been like her mother in the lifetime where she had pledged herself to be of service. Morgan was engulfed by a wave of love and adoration she had felt for The Morrighan in her past life.

"I am glad that you have just allowed yourself to feel the devotion that we have shared in the past. It is good that you voluntarily wish to honor the pledge that you made to me all those centuries ago. It is best not to resist. Allow yourself to accept what we are going to do tonight. I will enter your body and have a night of ardor and sexual gratification. You will enjoy it too."

A look of terror came over Morgan's face. "Am I getting this right? Are you saying that you want to take over my body and have sex with strangers?" Morgan started to pace back in forth in her towel.

The Morrighan started to get a bit perturbed when she saw Morgan's reaction. "Now, my dear, you will have fun too. There will not be any discomfort for you, only pleasure. Do not fear about what the men will do. When we find suitable specimens, I will take over their minds. They will only do as I wish them to do. They will not hurt you or do anything that would be disagreeable." The laugh. The chilling laugh.

Morgan could not abide by this idea. "I don't want to have sex with strange men," she thought.

"But my dear that was one of your primary roles when you served me as a priestess. You never became attached to the seed carriers. Why is that important now?" The green eyed specter asked with true curiosity in her voice.

A fit of passion came upon Morgan. It all came together instantaneously from deep within her. She decided to make a stand for herself. "Those priestess days are long gone. I will honor my commitment to fight for you. I am laying down my life for you. It that not enough for you?" Morgan asked with true sincerity in her voice.

The Morrighan grinned and the whole room became a deeper shade of emerald. "I understand your feelings and thoughts. Even though you did this for me many times in the past, I realize that now is a different time. You have not been properly trained to be in my service." The Morrighan floated around the room, thinking of how to deal with her perplexing priestess.

"Your vow is to serve me in any way that I wish," stated the emerald vixen. "I know that these concepts are strange to you. I will be kind to you and will not punish you for your impertinence this time. I know that you were never even told about me. That was your mother's duty when you became a woman. She was to have told you at your flowering ceremony. Yet this modern age does not understand the goddess or even honor us. Tonight I will have my pleasure. I will cloud your memory, so that you will not remember. "

Morgan started to cry. "How can this be happening?" she thought" Is this a bad dream? A nightmare?"

"No Morgan, this is not a dream. It is really happening at this time. I know all that you think, feel and do. We are connected by the water. When you are around water, our connection is amplified. The water energizes me and you. I will not attempt to educate you anymore now. Tonight we will have some entertainment."

Morgan was angry. She started to pace back and forth again.

"Do not wear yourself out, my dear. You will have a great time of it. It will be good for you. You will not feel frustrated any more. This infatuation you have for your teacher, Felipe, is distracting you from your task at hand. That is why you need this romp. You will feel much better, more grounded and

179

centered for the work that is ahead of you once this tension is released."

Suddenly, Morgan felt the urge to kneel in front of The Morrighan. Morgan fell to her knees and bowed her head to the earth. "Oh great Morrighan, please do not force me to fulfill your desires. I do have feelings for Felipe. I cannot share my body with another man right now. Even if you blank my mind during the experience, my body will know. This will just bring more painful feelings to me. That is not good for me and the task at hand. At another time, I might want to do that, but now I have to honor myself and the emotions within me."

Then Morgan stood up and suddenly she knew how to approach The Morrighan. "I am doing your bidding in ridding the world of this scum bag magician. Allow me something that is my own: the right to only share my body with the man who has my heart. PLEASE grant me this. I am doing so much. Please do not take away the sliver of happiness that I feel now. I need it to keep going. He makes me forget what is ahead of me. Please show me mercy this time."

Morgan had a sense that responding with hostility to an entity whose middle name is fury would not be the way to success. It was as if other parts of her were taking over and interacting with The Morrighan in a way that Morgan must have learned in her life as her priestess. Somehow Morgan knew that appealing to the "soft side" of this sinister deity would be the way to work with her. Morgan took a deep breath and let herself be engulfed in the love that she felt for Felipe. She let The Morrighan feel her love. Morgan also had a sense that The Morrighan knew that she was right. Morgan needed Felipe's love to keep going.

"Grant me this boon, Oh Phantom Queen, and allow me to keep that love in my heart pure and strong at this time. It gives me the motivation to fight and win. I have someone to come back to. My love for him is giving me a reason to live."

"You are wise, my child. I now understand how this love can benefit your mission. I will honor your request this time. I understand now that your love is a strong force within you. This fixation on love is important to people of this era, I see. I do have other priestesses who enjoy this experience and are not encumbered by the emotions that surround you at present." Then in a furry of green smoke, the apparition disappeared.

Morgan collapsed on the bed. She started to cry uncontrollably. Having to speak the words made her realize how much she felt for Felipe. She was not able to keep them locked away from her conscious mind anymore. She cried until she was exhausted. Then she soon fell sound asleep. As Morgan entered the dream state for the first time that night, she was happy to see her grandmother waiting for her at the edge of a great forest. Her grandmother embraced her as she ran into her arms. Morgan let out all of her frustration as she cried within her grandma's embrace. The wise old woman just stroked her hair until Morgan's crying fit subsided.

"I can't do what they want me to do, grandma!" Morgan whimpered.

"You just need practice. You have already learned what you need to succeed at this game. Remember when you were little and you would go into the essence of the trees? That is all you have to do. You know how. Just see yourself going with the ball as you send it into the goal ring, after you hit it with your hip. Guide the ball into the stone ring with your soul essence. Let that part of you do the work. Don't depend solely on the action of your physical body. See your spirit taking the ball into the stone circle. It is the same as when you went into the trees. It was so easy for you to float into the trees when you were little. You only need to get in touch with the wisdom and experience that is already inside you. Do not fear. You will play the game better than a Mayan! I know that you will make your mother and me proud." Grandma kissed Morgan on the cheek, turned and walked into the forest and disappeared.

"Grandmaaaaaaa" Morgan yelled as she awoke suddenly. Then she remembered what her grandmother had said in the dream. Morgan's mind quickly located the memories of her grandmother teaching her to go into the trees. In a few moments she looked down at the yellow dress she had on the day she first sailed into a tree trunk. As she relived the memory, she felt the denseness of the tree's body and the blissful joy she felt being inside a tree. As the memory faded, she laid back down on the bed, let out three shorts breaths and put her hands on her heart. She fell back into a dreamless sleep.

Visions Of Love

The days of February passed quickly. Morgan was able to use her grandmother's lesson of going into the essence of the trees to get the rubber ball through the stone circle of the handball court. She remembered that her grandmother had told her that connecting your soul essence to that of the tree was an ancient Druid practice.

It only took her a week of daily practice to get the technique to work at her will. Felipe did not know what had come over her to bring about such a big change in her performance. Her body was now acting like an incredible, synchronized machine. He sensed it was best not to question her. "I don't want to get her off course by asking what brought about this change. I am just thankful that she has been able to adjust and perform." He just sent out a silent prayer of thanks each day to the Holy Mother before they stepped into the stone circle at Boca Negra.

"Felipe is still acting like a snowman," Morgan thought one day as he walked in front of her to the stone circle that faithfully transported them to the Underworld. "He is still being distant and formal," she supposed as she looked away. His body seemed more appealing every day even though he was being more and more inaccessible each day.

Morgan disliked working with Bevis and Butthead, her names for Enrique and Eduardo. After a successful week, Felipe had told Concha that they could come to see her progress. This was the first time they had all been back in the Underworld. After a short time in the Underworld, the bored boys became fixated on Morgan's body. The potions and the memories of their sexual jaunts with Concha in the Underworld were definitely accelerating their sex drives. Morgan could feel them undressing her mentally. She just ignored it and went on. The raven haired beauty was used to getting attention that she did not desire. She realized that she had never heard a man's thoughts of her as clearly as in the Underworld.

Suddenly Felipe reached his breaking point. The Hispanic gentleman could no longer tolerate the rudeness and the perverted, sexual thoughts that Enrique and Eduardo kept spewing out, in English and Spanish, on the handball court. A fit of rage came over Felipe. "I have had enough of you pigs" he blasted mentally. The boys were shocked by his response. Morgan was delighted.

"He's standing up for me!" The mixture of feelings Morgan was experiencing translated into getting the rubber ball, hitting it with her hip and sending it right at Enrique's head. The surprised Enrique was hit right on the temple. "I have put up with your slimy remarks long enough!" she yelled mentally to Enrique.

Felipe was flabbergasted. In a fit of unexpected vigor, he commanded Concha's live- ins to leave. "See!" he said to Enrique "She knows how to move the ball around better then you two. Tell that to Concha and get out of here." The two young men acted like puppy dogs with their tails between their legs as they went to the stone cross and hurriedly disappeared.

Morgan was elated. Felipe was fuming. "And you!!!!" he looked at her with steel blue eyes that were now like laser beams, they were sending out so much force. "You still need more practice!" He turned his back on her and floated toward the cuadrafoil. "That is enough for today. Let's go!" He motioned her to go to the cross and she instantly disappeared. He soon followed.

After the now familiar sensations of traveling to and fro in the mysterious portal subsided, Morgan was standing in the stone ring of Boca Negra. Felipe helped her off with the handball regalia in agitated silence. They were both quiet as they drove back to Concha's house. It had become Morgan's gloomy jail when Felipe was not around. When they arrived at the entrance to her room, Felipe opened the door for her to walk through. After she walked into the room, she turned around to look at him. Quickly, without looking at her, he slammed the door shut with a loud bang. Morgan was greeted by the closed door in her face. In a few moments she heard his truck start up. She knew he was gone for the day.

"I don't know if he cares or if he was just pissed off at Enrique's rudeness," Morgan thought as she stepped out of the shower. She dried off, took another towel and wrapped it around herself. She went to the bed and lay down on top of it. "I like these times after taking the potion. It does give me visions."

A few moments after she closed her eyes, she started to get impressions. In a few seconds she became aware that she was getting information about her father who she had never known. She saw a ship, a large cargo vessel, which traveled back and forth across the Atlantic. She saw her mother, dressed as a waitress, in a coffee shop near the dock. Morgan could see the Statue of Liberty in the background and realized that the scene was in New York. Then she saw a man come in. He had black hair and green eyes. Morgan sensed that he was Irish. Morgan saw a green aura around him as he went into the eatery and sat down at the counter for some breakfast. Morgan realized that the green aura meant that he was the chosen mate for her mother. Then she saw her mother come up to the man and their energy fields joined in that instant. "I am seeing my mom and dad fall in love" she thought to herself. Then another scene appeared. The lovers were in a small bedroom. Her father was saying good-by and her mother was crying. "My mother never had a chance to share her life with my father. She never talked about him. I understand why now. There was nothing to talk about. I guess he was meant to be my sire, not my parent."

After the scene faded, Morgan could hear The Morrighan speaking to her. "You see, my dear, your mother and father never had a life together. That is not the way of the priestess. Your mother lived a convent-type life. She stayed with women, your grandmother and at times other priestesses. That was her family. The women in service to the goddess were always a close, loving group. They were able to help and comfort each other when they longed for a simpler life."

Morgan sat up in the bed and reflected upon what she had just witnessed. "She is helping me to fill in the blanks of my childhood."

"This is the way that it is, was and always will be." The Morrighan continued her lesson. "You will always have this type of life when you incarnate. That is one of the reasons why your marriage dissolved. Yours is a life of dedication to a cause. Particularly in these new times, your service is important not just to me and Ireland, but to the world. You have served other goddesses in different incarnations. For the most part, a goddess allows those dedicated to her to experience incarnations in the service of other goddesses. You came to know Ix Chel in another life. It is no coincidence that you washed up on her shore."

This thought opened up many others for Morgan. She suddenly realized that The Morrighan could be compassionate and generous. The Phantom Queen was what might be called dark, but she was not evil. "There is a difference, my dear, between dark and evil." The Morrighan whispered as she conversed with Morgan in her mind. "It is imperative for you to learn the teachings of our sect if you are to carry on the work." The Morrighan said in a very kind, loving tone. "I and my priestesses provide an important service that maintains the balance of this world. Not all worlds are such as this. When you have become skilled, you will have even greater understanding and have even greater travels in this world and others." Morgan decided not to react or evaluate this information but to be respectful of what The Morrighan was saying.

"We provide a service to this planet. The dark must be strong as well as the light. As a guardian of the shadow energy, I must contribute to maintaining the balance of living and dead here. I call those who need to go to their end. I allow their souls to leave their bodies so that they may go to their guides and teachers in the frequencies of spirit. All need to learn the lessons that this planet has to teach them. I am the one that calls back the wounded, the tired and the sick to return to the Source. I help them to release the cares of the body, to shed the traumas of living in this barbaric world." This last statement brought tears to Morgan's eyes.

"Humans seek the quiet and peace of the night when they have been too traumatized by living. I give healing and peace. I take my children back when they are done here. We give release and the way to start anew, to live again." Morgan was beginning to be impressed with The Morrighan. She was beginning to lose her fear of the specter. "Yes, Morgan, you are helping to maintain the balance of dark and light here. The Mayan midget has impaired the balance of death and rebirth in this part of the planet. The magician is evil. He takes life for selfish reasons: for his own lust and to keep on living well after his time on this earth should have ended. That is the trouble with those born of magic. It is always complicated to demolish them.

He is destroying the balance of dark and light energy in this world. That is why you have been called into service correct this imbalance. You are here to repair the balance of life and death on this world."

Morgan smiled and sensed the love that The Morrighan had for her. She felt the affection of all the women who had been in her life. The ex-trophy wife also felt the scope of the gargantuan task before her.

"Pleasant dreams, Morgan. You are going through life altering trials. The end result is that you will be brought back into balance and be in accord with who you truly are." The Morrighan had left her mind as smoothly as she entered. Morgan was able to bring up the face of her grandmother before she drifted into sleep.

Holy Mother

"We are going to Mexico City today," Felipe said as he walked into her room. If he had been an ice berg before, he was now like the empty, vast plains of the Arctic. "It is the Wayub time. Concha and her lads are in hiding near Uxmal. It is an old Mayan tradition. These five days, which usually come at the beginning of March, mark the end of the Mayan solar calendar, the Haab. This calendar is different from the astrology calendar, the Tzolkin. The Mayans had many calendars. The Haab is similar to our year calendar. It has five extra days between the old and New Year.

The Mayans considered these five days unlucky or unfortunate. It is when the Mayas let go of the past year and waited for the gods to bring the next year. No cooking is to be done, No new projects started. Everyone goes inside their homes and spends the time in silence and prayer. They contemplate what happened in the year that has ended and think about what they want to do in the coming year," he stated in the tone of a professor.

"It is nice that the Mayans have respect for the passing of the old and the bringing of the next year," Morgan added.

"It is really fear, not respect. They are frightened of offending the Mayan gods. They show their submissiveness to the Mayan deities by not carrying on business as usual."

"You seem to know a lot about the Mayan religion." Morgan said as they got into his old truck.

"I understand the old Mayan gods, but I do not worship them all. There is only one Mayan goddess to which I am devoted. That is Ix Chel, the Mother goddess of the Maya. Then there is Mother Mary, The Virgin of Guadalupe. The Holy Mother is probably the most powerful goddess on the planet right now. "Felipe said. "She is the goddess that we are going to see when we go to Mexico City. You need to pay homage to her, Morgan. She is strong. I cannot say if she is more commanding then the goddess that you serve, The Morrigahan. It is not for me to judge." Felipe was very respectful. Morgan got the sense that Felipe knew that The Morrighan was listening. She sensed that he did not want to offend the Irish specter.

"You need to enlist the aid of Mother Mary. It is always good to have all the assistance that you can get, especially in a situation such as this," Felipe said. "Now gather your things together. You don't need to bring clothes. I have brought you this red wig. It will disguise you for the plane ride to Mexico City and for all the walking around that we have to do. Don't forget your hat." From out of his large back pack, Felipe pulled a shoulder length wig of straight, red hair. He handed it to Morgan with a chuckle. "People may still recognize you even though your picture has been out of the news for a while. Put the wig on when we get out of sight.

I don't want the guard to see that anything is different. You have been very sheltered here, but now we must venture out into the world, to see Mother Mary. I know that she will help you." With her red wig and her floppy hat stuffed into her large bag that had been with her through so much, Morgan was prepared to go on a trip.

"It will be nice to have a change of scenery," Morgan said as she walked through the door of her room. When Felipe closed the door to Morgan's detention center behind him, Felipe rattled off some phrases in Spanish to the guard, who instantly laughed robustly.

"What did you tell him?" Morgan asked as they walked to his truck.

"That I am taking you to my house to make love to you so you will relax," Felipe said without smiling. "We're going to the airport" he said once she was in his truck. "The plane ride to Mexico City will be about an hour and a half. We will be staying in Mexico City for two nights. We will visit with my sister," he said as he closed the door on Morgan's side of his truck. He went around to the other side and let himself in. They rode back to Lupe and Felipe's house without any discussion. He parked his truck next to a blue door. "Put your wig on," Felipe ordered, as he went through the blue door. Morgan stayed in the car and put the wig on. She looked in the rear view mirror to see if it was on straight. When Morgan saw her reflection, she realized that she looked just like her mother. This actually brought tears to her eyes. Felipe came back out in a few moments with a back pack that was very full.

There was a taxi waiting in front of the yellow door, the main entrance to the hacienda. Felipe escorted her to the taxi and opened the door. Morgan slid on to the taxi's back seat and Felipe glided next to her. He got very close. This made Morgan break out in a big smile.

"Maybe he will start being nice to me?" she thought as she stared into his azure eyes.

Once he got closer, he cleared his throat and then continued to talk in his serious tone. "I must tell you about the Virgin of Guadalupe. I assume, since your heritage is Irish, that you are a catholic?

Morgan nodded her head to say no. "I never went to church. My family was very spiritual, but not in the way of organized religion. I learned to worship Nature like the ancient Druids." Morgan said "Especially the element of water. I understand now why my mother and grandmother always felt that water was sacred. They had special jars of water from all over the world. Some was holy water from churches, some from extraordinary places. My mother and grandmother would do ceremonies several days a year. The water was always a very important part of those rites. "Morgan stopped for a moment and then reflected. "I see now that it is a sacred element."

"I thought as much. Most goddesses are connected to some element or other. Yours Is definitely, the water. Ix Chel is also connected to water."

Morgan nodded in agreement as she put on the sun glasses that Felipe was holding out to her. Even though it was grey and overcast at the ocean, Felipe made it clear, without saying a word that she needed to wear these glasses while they were out in public. Or did Morgan just know this? Was she reading his mind? She felt like she was. "Do I feel closer to him because I am falling in love with him, or is it just the combination of the potions and the work that we are doing?" After a moment of thought Morgan realized that she did not want to analyze it too much. She knew that she was attuning to him on many levels. She knew that they were coming closer and that is all that mattered to her at this moment. She was just enjoying being in the glow of his joie de vivre. She loved the smell of his hair, and the roughness of his beard.

"We are going to the airport at Cancun, and from there we will take a direct flight to Mexico City. Then we will go to my sister's house in the Zona Rosa. We will return before the five day Wayub period is over and Concha comes out of her seclusion. We cannot risk her getting suspicious. I don't want her to think that I am helping you more then she wants me to." He sat back and thought for a bit. "We are going to Mexico City to enlist the help of the Holy Virgin. With her on your side, you will succeed," Felipe said with conviction.

Morgan just smiled at Felipe. She was enjoying his attention. He had been so stern and remote, lately. "I hope we can have some fun on this trip," Morgan thought to herself. She chuckled and thought "What might be fun? Hugs and kisses? Passionate sex? Sleeping with his arms around her all night? All of the above!" She yelled out in her mind.

Felipe moved so that his body was touching Morgan as the taxi started toward the Cancun airport. "Wow, he is coming close to me!" Morgan tried to keep her squeal of joy inside herself, not let it out for him to hear. She was trying to look detached as he moved into position so that he could speak easily into her   ear.

"I must tell you about the Virgin," he said with a serious tone in his voice. He was talking in a loud whisper. "I do not want the taxi driver hear me." Felipe said as he started to relate the story of how the Virgin of Guadalupe came to this continent. "We are going to the church of Tepeyec that was built for the Holy Virgin," he said with a tone of reverence in his voice.

"Mother Mary first came to this continent shortly after it had been invaded by Cortez. It was the year 1531. The Indians had been tormented and tortured by the Spanish intruders. Cortez and his soldiers took over and desecrated many of the places of worship that existed here. They tried to get the Mayans to worship Jesus by building churches over their existing temples and pyramid,." he said as she sunk back into the taxi cab seat. "I want to tell you this from my heart. My heart is so full of love for the Holy Mother." Morgan could feel the sentiment in his voice. This brought out even more feelings within her that translated to new appreciation of his devotion.

"Mother Mary appeared to a farmer named Juan Diego, in December of that year. He was walking on a barren hill, called Tepeyec, near Mexico City. Mother Mary appeared to him there. She told him to go to the local bishop and tell him that she wanted a church built, dedicated to her, on this spot. In this very area was the shrine that had been destroyed by the Spanish. It had been dedicated to the Aztec goddess Tonanstin. She was the goddess of childbirth and the moon cycles. She was very similar to IX Chel, the Mayan goddess."

"The farmer went back to the bishop and told him of the Holy Mother's desire. The bishop did not believe the farmer. He wanted some proof that Mother Mary had actually been there. He did not want to take the man's word for all of this, even though the man was very dedicated to the new religion that had come to his land. The bishop told Juan to get evidence from Mother Mary. Juan went back to the spot, which was a cold and barren hill. It was the middle of December. Yet there, on Tepeyec Hill, was a bush that was in full bloom with red Castilian roses. "

"That is amazing." Morgan interjected.

"The farmer brought the roses back to the bishop. He picked them and wrapped them up in his poncho. When he opened the cape in front of the bishop, not only did the roses fall to the ground, but a painting of Mother Mary was imprinted on the cape."

"A true miracle." Morgan added quietly, with a tone of reverence in her voice.

Felipe had a hint of a grin on his face as he pulled out the gold medallion, on a gold chain, from under his sweater. "She understands," Felipe thought to himself. Just knowing that Morgan was able to open her heart to accept this knowledge gave him an overwhelming sense of peace.

"Yes Morgan that was just the start of the miracles that Mother Mary brought with her presence here. The robe now hangs in the church of Tepeyec. The painting has been copied many times and has many versions." His pendant had a picture of the Virgin of Guadelupe on it. "This is an exact replica of the picture that appeared on Juan Diego's poncho."

Morgan took it in her hand and looked at it for a few moments. Her hand that held the medallion stated to get hot. Morgan could feel tingling in her hand as well. She was also impressed with the detail of the image that was before her. It reminded Morgan of many of the classical European pictures that were drawn of Jesus and Mother Mary in Europe.

"When the bishop saw not only the roses but also the painting," Felipe continued, "he could no longer doubt. He fell to his knees and promised that he would build the church for the Holy Mother. After this event, Juan Diego wanted to go see his Uncle, who was close to death. When he arrived at his uncle's home, he found his uncle completely well. That was the second miracle that the Holy Mother did. The third one happened after the church was built. There was a celebration with the Indians and the Spanish at the new church that had been built for Mother Mary. During the festivities, one of the Indian men was accidently shot in the neck with an arrow. He had died instantly. His body was laid out on the ground before the altar, in front of the poncho with the painting of the Virgin of Guadalupe. Then another miracle happened. The man was suddenly healed. He got up and walked away in a few minutes."

Morgan eyes started to fill with tears as she closed them. They streamed down her cheeks. She inhaled and exhaled deeply as she grasped the profundity of what Felipe was sharing with her. She was going to see the drawing of Mother Mary, as she had made herself known to the people of this continent. The energy of what he was saying seemed to engulf her. Morgan was filled with appreciation as she lay her head on Felipe's shoulder and whispered a sincere" Thank you for doing this for me," in his ear. Felipe patted her head and then moved away a little bit.

"Yes, Morgan" he said clearing his throat, "The Holy Virgin was later to unite the Indians in their battle for independence from Spain. She became a symbol that is very strong within the hearts of all Mexicanos today." Felipe stated as he cleared his throat a few more times and moved to the other side of the taxi. Morgan instantly felt a change in his spirit. She could actually feel his energy field shrink as he moved away.

"Oh, no" Morgan thought "I thought it was going so well, and now he is pulling back from me again!" She felt the gloom of his rejection come over her. "I guess I am not used to men rejecting me," she thought as she sank deeper into the seat of the taxi.

"We are almost at the airport, Morgan." Felipe stated. "We will be getting out and moving fast. Hold on to my hand. We will be moving quickly to reach the boarding gate." Felipe announced.

Felipe opened her door and helped her step on to the sidewalk. She saw waves of brightly colored people moving in different directions as she left the calmness of the taxi. She held on tightly to Felipe's hand as they made their way through the bustling airport. Fortunately, Felipe had timed their arrival so that they did not have to wait very long at the airport.

Once Morgan was sitting in the window seat of the small plane, she began to unwind. She had felt that there were many eyes on her as she walked through the airport. "I need to relax. The last few weeks have been so trying," she thought to herself. "Learning to play the handball game has been a challenge. Even so, I am getting pretty good at it." Her natural grace and coordination, combined with grandma's 'connecting with the trees' concept was working nicely. Now Morgan could move the weighty, rubber orb around the Underworld like it was a ping pong ball.

"You are getting better at the game," Felipe said as the plane was starting to take off.

Morgan sat up with a start. "Is this guy reading my mind" she though. "Thanks," she answered in a surprised tone. "I find that I enjoy it." Again she marveled at the mental synchronicity between them that got stronger each day.

"We need to perfect your blocking. That is also an important part of the game. It is necessary to keep Ixma from getting the ball through his ring. You need to be sharp when you battle Ixma. He will be weak from not feeding, but he still knows the game. He watched many while Uxmal was in its prime. "

"Well, I know that I will beat him. My life depends on it."

That last statement hit a nerve. Felipe instantly got a serious look on his face and sat back in his aisle seat. Morgan could sense his trepidation. "You might want to take a nap while the plane is moving. Put the hat over your face, so people will not be able to recognize you while sleeping."

"I guess that I am wearing on you" Morgan said with a laugh that was not filled with happiness.

"This is a grave situation, Morgan. I cannot help but worry. You are prepared in many ways, but it is still a challenge that demands that you work with the customs that are not familiar to you. It will take all that you have within you to slay the magician. That is why we need to ask for the help of the Holy Mother. She may be able to aid you in ways that The Morrighan cannot," he said as he sank into his seat and waited for the plane to take off.

As the plane left the asphalt, he closed his eyes. She did the same. She put the hat with the floppy brim over her face and got as comfortable as possible to doze off. He had given her a lot to think about. It didn't take long before she fell asleep. The plane took off smoothly and in a few moments both slipped into a light slumber. They both awoke as the plane touched down in Mexico City.

Once they were off the plane, they were engulfed by an undulating wall of people. The Mexico City airport was very busy. Fortunately with her wig, sunglasses and hat, Morgan attracted little attention. "It is good that no one recognizes you," Felipe murmured under his breath." This airport gets a lot of international travelers and many of the people in this part of the country have blood ties to Europe and Spain. You don't stick out as much." Morgan looked around at the rivers of passing people and realized he was right. She kept her head down, held on to Felipe's hand and walked through the airport. She could not see where she was going, so she kept a tight grip.

"At least he is touching my hand," Morgan thought to herself as they walked to the taxi stand.

Felipe opened the door of a waiting taxi and ushered Morgan into the back seat. He got in after her.

"85 Calle Hidalgo," he said to the driver. Once they were sitting in the taxi, Morgan wanted to take off the glasses. Felipe made a swift gesture to her arm to tell her that she must not take off the glasses. Morgan sank back into the taxi seat. After a few moments, Felipe said "This is called the Zona Rosa, the pink zone. It is the most exquisite part of Mexico City" he said. Through her glasses, Morgan could see the shop lined streets and many well-dressed people strolling upon them.

"It has a distinct European quality" Morgan said back, showing off a bit of her art history.

"Mexico city was settled by the Spanish, so it does have that air to it. These buildings are very old, from the 1600's.

"We are coming into the residential part of the Zona Rosa," Felipe said to her as the taxi turned off the main street. The taxi ambled by lush, overgrown gardens that peeked out from behind high walls.

"It is very interesting that all the walls have glass and barbed wire at the tops," Morgan said She was used to security at her homes, but this took it to another level.

"Mexico City has become a very dangerous place, Morgan. People like you get kidnapped all the time. Even people like my sister and her family, to whose house we are going, has to be very careful," he said in a serious tone.

Felipe got out of the taxi in front of a large gate. A manor could be seen in the background that appeared to have several stories. Felipe hit the bell at the side of the gate. "Hola, es Felipe," he said. The gate responded by opening. Felipe hurriedly reentered the taxi before it meandered through the lush, well-manicured entry garden of the estate. Morgan got a long look at the three stories of the colonial style manor that had been painted in deep shades of tan. The tall, French windows throughout the dwelling were draped with rich satins of rust and forest green that could be seen on the duo's unhurried ride up the circular driveway. Morgan was unintentionally holding her breath as she rode up to a mansion that exceeded the grandeur of many of the De Armond estates.

It was early afternoon when the taxi let them off at the front door. Felipe started to laugh as they walked closer to the front door. "You can take off your glasses now, Morgan," he said with a laugh.

"Buenos Tardes, Senor Felipe. I will tell mistress that you are here," the attractive young maid said with a smile after she opened the door to greet them. She opened the door as wide as it would go and stood back to give them plenty of room to enter the mansion. Morgan could see past the maid into the entrance way of the vast house. She saw Louis 14th furniture, crystal chandeliers, tapestries and European paintings on the walls. Large arrangements of fresh flowers were everywhere.

Felipe gestured for Morgan to enter the house. Morgan stood in the foyer. Felipe moved past her into the home. She followed him up a circular stairway, down a long hall to a suite with a high ceiling and exquisite décor that matched the window treatments. There was a drawling room area that had a grand piano, a magnificently ornate fireplace spectacular couches and tables and an entertainment center that had to be 30 feet wide. Morgan was walking around the room, carefully looking at all the antiques.

"My little sister had done well. She made a good marriage, as you can see. I grew up in a family that is part of Mexican high society."

Morgan nodded her head. "Yes, I would say."

"You must be familiar with this type of life," Felipe said. "When my Shaman's Death started, it was all taken away from me," he added. " I have no regrets. I wouldn't have met you If I would have stayed in Mexico City, now would I?" he added with a grin and a chuckle.

"A little acknowledgement. Maybe he does care for me," she mused as she looked at a vase and tried to remember what period it was from.

Then Felipe's sister appeared at the doorway. "Good afternoon, Morgan" said the impeccably groomed, tall, slender women in her late 30's. She was dressed conservatively yet with great elegance. Morgan mused that she looked as if she had been a model in Vogue.

"It is my honor to have you in my home, Morgan" the woman said. "My name is Miranda. I am pleased to meet you." She held out her hand and Morgan met it with hers. After they shook hands, Miranda said "We will have dinner in about an hour." With that she left the room and left her older brother with Morgan.

"You are not overwhelmed with all this luxury, are you Morgan?" Felipe asked.

"No." Morgan replied. "I didn't think that you were connected to such wealth," she stated. "You seem to be so unaffected by worldly things," Morgan said with all sincerity. "It must have been hard to leave it all" she added.

"No, not after my Shaman's death started. It was change or be killed," he replied. "I will tell you about it sometime," he said as he showed her through her quarters. He opened up the large armoire that housed not only a tv and music system , but also had a small refrigerator and shelves of delicacies like French chocolates, croissants, fresh fruits and other types of Mexican pastries. "There are some clothes in there." Felipe said as he motioned toward the adjoining sleeping area. As Morgan entered the bedroom she gasped at the splendor of the four-poster bed that was covered with a cut velvet comforter and linens of deep hues of green. A nearby chaise lounge reflected the terra cotta and jade color scheme. The table and chairs, obviously for writing or computer usage, were fashioned from rich Mahogany wood. Overstuffed chairs and a plush window seat completed the sleeping area.

Why don't you take a hot bath and change? I will knock on the door when dinner is ready," he stated as he closed the door behind him.

Morgan stripped and headed to the bathroom within her elegant chamber.

"Yeah, I am ready for this" she thought as she sank her body into the oversized, copper tub that was complete with Jacuzzi jets. "A nice soak and a nap," she thought as rested her head on the side of the tub and let herself slip into the darkness.

The knock on the door startled Morgan awake. She had fallen asleep in the tub. The knock scared her. She quickly, got out of the tub and pulled a towel around her. "Yes?"

"Please get dressed Morgan," said the familiar male voice. "I will meet you at the foot of the stairs in 15 minutes."

Morgan got up and sauntered into the walk in closet that was larger than her whole room at Concha's place. It has dresses, pants, light sweaters and blouses neatly hanging from the racks in the center of the room. There was a whole wall of shoes on one side of the closet. Purses, hats, belts and other accessories filled out the other walls of the u shaped clothing heaven. Morgan looked through the clothes and picked a form fitting, floor length cerulean blue dress. It had matching shoes. "I feel like I just went shopping," Morgan laughed as she put on her attire and then left the room.

At the foot of the stairs stood Felipe. A different Felipe. Gone were the jeans and tee shirts. He was wearing a dark grey dress suit, pale blue shirt and striped blue tie. "The shirt and tie make the color of his eyes really pop," Morgan mused. Morgan also chuckled to herself to see that they were wearing the same colors. Their synchronicity was startling and at the same time pleasant to her.

The dinner was elegant, polite and very formal. Morgan felt thankful to have a safe, comfortable place. She found that she fully enjoyed the assortment of delectable cuisine that was on display. The meal offered both American and Hispanic foods. There were also several types of beer, wine and liquor. Morgan thought back to some of the sumptuous banquets she had attended as Mrs. De Armond. This meal was equal to those and had the added flavors of the Latin world.

"Thank you for opening your home to me," Morgan said to Miranda. "You have a lovely home and you are a great hostess," she stated with a sincere heart. Morgan suddenly realized that this woman was trapped, just as she had been. "She has to go through the motions, but is really seeking something else," Morgan sensed. Morgan realized that she was tuning into Miranda and picking up her deepest sentiments. Morgan had the awareness that these were feelings that Miranda did not want anyone to know. "I think I am becoming more psychic," Morgan reflected to herself as she finished the delectable meal.

When they were finished, Felipe was the one who took charge of the evening. He escorted her to her bedroom. He stopped outside the door and turned to face her. "Morgan, I need to talk to you before you go to bed," he said in a serious voice. "You need to go to sleep now, even though it is early. We will get up very early, before dawn tomorrow. It is a long ride to the cathedral in Tepeyec, where the cloth of the Holy Virgin is kept. It is best to go early, before the city wakes up. You clothes for tomorrow have been laid out for you. Go to sleep, now," he instructed as he started to walk away.

Morgan felt deserted again. "Felipe," Morgan yelled after him. "Before we go to bed, would you tell me about your Shaman's Death? I guess I would like to hear what someone else has gone through." Morgan was not used to sleeping so early in the evening. She wanted to talk a bit with Felipe before she was remanded to her bedroom for the evening.

Felipe took in a deep breath, lowered his head, and then looked up into Morgan's eyes. "I was engaged to be married to the daughter of a high ranking Mexican diplomat. Two days before the wedding, we got into a car accident. I was driving. It was not my fault, but my fiancé died instantly. My life was threatened by her outraged family, and I had

209

to flee Mexico City. I knew that my fiancée's family would not kill me, but they were so enraged that I did not want to stay around to give them the opportunity to disfigure me as a memento of the accident. My family urged me to go to my uncle's home in the Yucatan. That took me out of sight of the vengeful eyes of her kinfolk.

Three days after I arrived in Playa Del Carmen, I had a dream of a man who was to become my teacher. A month later, I encountered him at a Mayan Winter Solstice ceremony near Merida. He was a spindly man of 70 who had blue eyes and a very long beard. I recognized him from my dream. He disappeared from the ceremony before I could come up to him. The dream made it clear that he was my teacher. I knew I had to find him. It took me two weeks of looking for him all over the city to finally find him sipping coffee at an outdoor café on the main plaza.

I was soon apprenticed to the elusive virtuoso. I spent three years learning to make healing poultices, sing healing chants and give lying on of hands to the sick and elderly. He shared his knowledge of the Mayan traditions including their astrology, ceremonies and curative practices. A week before he died, he gave me several of the Mayan artifacts that had been entrusted to him from his teachers. That is how my spiritual path began. I am sure that when it is time, I will find the next person who is meant to be the guardian of this knowledge." Felipe gave her a smile that was laced with the pain of the past. "Now rest."

Morgan was in a pensive mood as she got naked and slipped between the satin sheets. The knowledge of Felipe's past had touched her profoundly. She had even greater appreciation for him. She felt that she had met someone who had gone through what she was now experiencing. It gave her comfort. She now thought of Felipe as a comrade in this situation and not only a teacher.

Morgan had a tough night. She tossed and turned most of the night. She had snippets of dreams where she was fighting an ugly, black monster. In other dreams she found herself kneeling at an altar in a cave and another where she was following a monkey, trying to catch him but never being able to grasp his tale.

"Wake up, Morgan," she heard Felipe's voice and felt his arms on her shoulders. She opened her eyes to see the handsome Latino standing over her. When her eyes fixed upon his, he smiled and left the room. Jeans, a sweat shirt, an ash blond wig and a hat were waiting on a nearby table. In a few minutes, she was dressed and ready for the day.

They closed the front door of the mansion behind them and walked out to the semicircular driveway where the taxi was waiting to take them to the church at Tepeyec. "It is very crowded in the city. It has the largest population of any city in the world," Felipe stated.

They arrived at a large church with a huge plaza in about a half hour. The two exited the taxi, and

Felipe settled with the driver. Morgan was not ready for what she experienced next. She was still half asleep. As soon as she walked through the church doors, all she could see was a bright gold light. "The light is almost blinding," she thought as she followed Felipe and they walked to the area where the cape, with the image of Mother Mary had been imprinted some 500 years earlier.

Morgan and Felipe walked in silence as they approached to the room that held the sacred relic. Soon they stood at the entrance to the room that held the cape that Juan Diego used to carry roses from Mother Mary. Morgan was in awe at the whole situation. She had never seen such a church. "I haven't been to many churches," she whispered to Felipe, "But this has the strongest energy of any church I have ever been in."

"Wait until you get in front of the cloth," Felipe said to her as he ushered her into the room where the holy relic was preserved behind glass. "The colors have not faded in over 500 years," Felipe stated as they stood in front of the image that had miraculously been imprinted upon the cloth. They were both taken in by the energy of the fabric. "Kneel." he said as he pulled her to the ground.

Morgan followed his instructions. "Keep your head down," she heard Felipe say. He was kneeling beside her.

Morgan sunk into a meditative prayer state right away. Then the vision started. Morgan was standing at the bottom of a Mayan pyramid. It was not the one at Uxmal; it was bigger. There was a long pathway with pyramids on both sides. Morgan found herself going to the one at the end of the walkway. She floated to the top of it. There was a beautiful woman waiting there. Morgan got the impression that she was pregnant. She had on a robe of gold underneath and a teal colored robe that also covered her head .She had light, coffee colored skin and brown eyes. She emitted a great deal of love and bliss. Then from under her cloak, she pulled out a black dagger. She said "Use it at the right time." The Holy Mother offered the dark blade to Morgan. She reached for the dagger with her left hand. The blade floated into her palm. Then the robed woman started to emit a golden radiance that encapsulated Morgan completely. She smiled at Morgan and the scene disappeared.

Morgan opened her eyes. She was a bit stunned by what she had just witnessed. "I had an incredible vision," she whispered to Felipe with the sweetness of Mother Mary still around her.

"Tell me later," he replied bluntly. Then he fell back into meditative silence.

Morgan found it easy to slip back into a light trance. She began to see snippets of scenes from the past. She saw the Holy Mother again, doing healings and appearing as white light in the darkness of night. "These are the miracles that have happened here. You will be saved like those you have seen," she heard a voice whisper in her head. Morgan did not look up. She did not move. She was held steadfast by the

213

visions that were passing before her inner sight. Tears started falling down her face as she knelt motionless. They stayed in front of the cloth for almost 20 minutes. It took that long for Morgan to stop crying. Then Felipe helped her up and held her by the arm as they walked to a bench in a waiting area of the church.

"What happened to you in there, Morgan?" he asked

"I don't know really. I just saw a lot of scenes flashing in my mind. Then a voice said that I would be saved."

"That is fantastic, Morgan," Felipe had tears in his eyes too.

"Did anything happen for you, Felipe?' Morgan asked innocently.

"Yes, but I cannot talk to you about it now," he said. He ushered her into the gift shop. He went to a counter and seemed to be looking for something specific. When he found it, he motioned Morgan to come to him. He talked to the sales lady, took some bills out of his wallet, paid for his gift and had her put it in a bag. "I am getting you a vile of holy water that you will be able to bring into the Underworld," he told her as they were walking out of the church. "You will be able to wear it around your neck during the handball game. I do not know if Mother Mary can come into the Underworld, but I know that she is with you. She has made her presence in your life clear. She has performed many miracles, so she will be able to handle this situation. It is time to go."

The day was beginning as they emerged from the dark womb of the church. Morgan could see hundreds of people going about their business in the large plaza. "We are going back to the house. It is not safe for you to be outside." Felipe said as he hailed a taxi. One came quickly and they sped back to his sister's mansion in the Zona Rosa. "My sister and I are two of four children. Our parents were involved in many political campaigns and have done very well financially because of that connection," he said as they got closer to his sister's house. "We had a great many opportunities as children. That is why I speak English," he said

"Perfect English," Morgan added with a smile. He grinned politely.

"I know that this may seem strange to you, but I am glad that I am away from this life. It always seemed like a life I didn't want. Now looking at it again, being here, I feel very good knowing that I have made the right decision," he said as the taxi stopped and he got out to open her door. "It is hard for me to be here. I haven't been back in many years. It is forcing me to heal many of my old issues. It has been good for me to reconnect with my sister. " He smiled and lowered his head as she exited the taxi.

"I am glad that this trip is helping you too," she said and thought to herself. "He is so sensitive. It makes me love him even more." Morgan stopped when she heard her thoughts. Part of her was shocked at what she had just heard in her mind. "Wow, I guess I do love him." She lowered her head as well. It had been a very intense day.

When they returned to the mansion, Felipe turned to her." We will have lunch in a couple of hours. Would you like to take a swim in the pool?"

Morgan shook her head "Yes." Then she said, "I don't have a swim suit."

"There are many in your room. I will meet you at your room in a few minutes." He escorted Morgan to her room. She gave him a timid smile and closed the door behind her.

She did find several swim suits in the chest of drawers across from the bed. After taking them all out and trying on many, she settled on a string bikini. "Yummy" she said as she looked at herself in the mirror in the bathroom. She put on a cover-up that she found in the drawers as well and then opened the door.

Felipe was standing outside her door, a towel wrapped around his waist. "Follow me," he stated quietly. Morgan watched him turn around and go in the direction of the indoor pool. Morgan followed Felipe through a maze of rooms until they ended up in front of a wrought iron door. They entered the luxurious pool area. It was painted with ocean scenes, had a hot tub, an Olympic size swimming pool and locker rooms. Felipe opened up his towel to reveal his learn, toned body clothed in conservative swim trunks. He laid it across an empty lounge chair and dived into the middle of the pool.

Morgan followed him in, entering the pool with graceful dive. When she came up for air, they both laughed heartily. For the first half hour they swam around the pool, splashed each other, and behaved like a couple of five year olds. "It's great to feel free and happy again. I do want to get back to myself" she thought. "But who am I really?" she asked herself. She certainly had a lot of choices: trophy wife, warrior priestess, midget slayer, freaked –out, clueless thirty year old. She had tried not to think about Gerard. She knew that there was great anger inside her for what he had done. Yet she didn't give herself the luxury of thinking negative thoughts about him. "I can't afford to dwell on anything but winning the game and killing the midget," she thought to herself.

"You are a great swimmer, Morgan," he said as he started to do the breast stroke across the pool. "I have noticed that when you play the handball game. You are very graceful and have a great sense of balance."

"Thank you," Morgan replied, with a very silky, coquettish tone in her voice. Felipe started to stiffen up. Morgan's girlish, playful manner acted like a blast of Arctic wind. Felipe started doing laps in the pool. Morgan got out of the pool and started to dry off. The thought "You messed it up again!!!!" started blaring in her mind.

"Are you leaving?" he asked.

"Yes, I think I have had enough for the moment. I am going to change for lunch. If I can't find my way back to my room, I will yell for help"

"There are servants everywhere, so just call out and they will be there," he said

When Morgan exited the pool room, he did not look up. He just kept doing laps. She was able to make it back to her room, where she fell on to the bed. Minus the bikini, she soon drifted into a light sleep. It seemed like only a few minutes when she woke to a knock at the door.

"Senora, the meal is ready," the maid announced.

She put on a robe and yelled "OK" through the door. She dressed quickly in cream colored silk slacks and matching print blouse that were in the closet. "I might as well look the part," she thought as she opened the door and went down stairs. Felipe was waiting for her. He looked very elegant. He now had on brown slacks and a mocha colored cardigan sweater that showed off his muscular chest. They were wearing the same colors again. Out of all the choices they both had, they picked almost identical colors schemes. This coincidence took Morgan aback. She smiled to herself as she accepted the connection that was getting stronger between them.

"I am famished. I hope you are too," he said in his polite tone of voice.

"I am ready to eat, that is for sure," Morgan replied in an enthusiastic tone. As Morgan walked into the dining room, she was amazed at the feast that was spread out before her. There were many types of Mexican foods: Buffet trays were filled with chili rellenos, burritos, enchiladas and chimichangos. There were also caviar, salmon, breads from all over the world as well as Asian dishes. At the far end of the buffet chocolate éclairs, cheesecakes, and countless pastries awaited. It was an incredible feast.

Morgan loaded up on the caviar and smoked salmon, but politely sampled many of the other dishes. "Thank you for having this incredible feast!" she said to Miranda, her husband and the three children that were also at the banquet.

"It is our pleasure. Thank you for bringing Felipe back to us." The two women locked eyes. Learning Felipe's story enabled Morgan to understand the depth of Miranda's words.

Morgan sat down at the far end of the long dining room table and waited for the others to serve themselves and be seated. Once everyone had their plate in front of them, Felipe led them in a prayer. "Thank you Mother Mary, your son Jesus and all the guides and teachers for bringing us together on this day. Thank you for all the gifts you sent to us and all the protection and healing you give us." They all said Amen and started to eat.

During the meal, Morgan chatted with Miranda's husband, Guillermo, and the children. She did know the unwritten laws of socializing. After an hour of eating and conversation had passed, Miranda stood and announced:

"It is our custom to take a nap after a large meal. The traditional Hispanic way is to eat well in the middle of the day and then take the famous Siesta and let the food digest. Pleasant dreams." She motioned for the children to rise and the dining room was soon evacuated. Morgan knew the way to her room. She graciously listened to the children's directions, smiled and headed up the stairway.

"I am really not sleepy," she thought to herself when she returned to her room. There was a television. She tried it for a while and then got bored with all the Spanish stations. There was a pile of magazines that she thumbed through. Finally a full stomach and the comfortable bed overtook her and she fell into a deep sleep.

It was dark when she awoke. "I think that I will go to the pool," she mused. "I feel so much better, stronger from just being in the pool." Felipe had told her that it was a salt water pool. That was heaven to Morgan. Since the night of the big bang with the magician she had come to relish the feelings that salt water gave her. She had to go swim in the pool again. She put on one of the suits, this time a one piece, and was very quiet as she went down the stairs. The pool room was completely dark when she entered. "So much the better," she thought. "I think that I am just going to take my suit off and float in the water in the dark." She slipped her nude body into the lukewarm salt water and found it easy to float on her back.

After floating for a few moments, visions started to come. She saw her mother in a field of thistles. Her mother was digging up the barren ground. Morgan got the impression that her mother was getting ready for Spring planting. The surroundings looked cold and bleak. Morgan had a sense that her mother was in Scotland or some very cold, barren place in Britain. Her mother realized that she was being watched, and turned to face Morgan.

"Morgan! You are on your first mission for the goddess. I know that what has happened to you has been very traumatic but you will …"

Suddenly the light went on. Morgan was shaken out of her trance. She was floating on her back, arms and legs spread apart. Felipe, totally naked, with just a towel over his shoulder, was standing there looking at her. He was surprised too. Surprised and aroused. He had an instantaneous erection just seeing Morgan's nude body floating, spread eagle, in the water. He was the one to turn red this time.

"Do you see the effect you have on me, Morgan?" he stated with a great deal of intensity in his voice. "Do you think that I have no feelings for you? Do you think that your body, your smell and the way your hair spirals down your back doesn't drive me crazy? Do you realize how hard it is for me to be with you every day and not be able to hold you and give you the pleasure that I feel you crave? I am tortured each

221

moment that I am around you. Yet I cannot act on my passion now."

He put the towel around his body, but his erection was not going away "I don't want to distract you from your mission. You need your entire focus on this battle. You cannot feel soft or loving. You must feel the disgust, the rage, the drive to win this challenge, no matter what you must do to achieve it. I will not let myself distract you in any way. I must know that you are fully focused on the task ahead of you. I recognize that you are feeling safe and comfortable now. But you must be ready in a couple weeks. You need to think of all the women who have lost their lives so you can put a stop to the senseless carnage. You have so much yet to do, and you need all your attention on the goal. That is why I have been so distant."

He said in a soft voice." When you are victorious, you will come to me and I will please you in ways that have been lost since the time of the ancient Maya. I will awaken your body to experience the satisfaction that you desire. Let that be the spoils of war. You are fighting a life and death battle. You must be ready." He walked out and turned the light out. Morgan was left alone in the dark. She kept floating for another hour, tears of joy streaming down her face and merging with the salty water.

On the way back to her quarters, she head flute music coming out of the room down the hall. She knew it was Felipe's room, for she had watched him go into it the night before. The exquisite, melancholy tones of the flute floated out into the corridor. The soulful music comforted her. She now knew his heart. Now she could fight because she knew that he loved her. She needed a reason to fight for her life.

The Countdown
March 19th

Morgan and Felipe were the first of the party of five to come through the portal at Boca Negra that day. "Did you see the way I ran circles around Butthead and kept getting the ball in the stone circle?" Morgan bubbled forth with laughter as she described the handball practice that had just ended.

"Eduardo, Morgan. His name is Eduardo!" Felipe stated firmly through his laughter. "Yes, you won again today. You certainly have mastered the game. Now be quiet. They will be coming through in a moment. Sit down and rest," Felipe commanded.

Morgan gave him the "Yes Master," look as she sat down on a rock. In less than a minute, the exotic Concha and her two lovers came through the portal into Boca Negra.

After a moment of shaking her body out and straightening out her form fitting leggings and skin tight tank top, Concha smiled happily at Morgan. "You play very good, my dear, I will tell Ixma you be ready on 21st." The three thousand year old woman walked slowly back to her car. She was beginning to feel the effects of having taken the life force of girls that were not yet mature. They did not have the mating hormones activated. This always attracted more life force to a woman's body. Concha tired, but needed to keep up the pretense for a few more days. She could not look at Morgan. Concha knew that she was the one who would relinquish her life so that Concha could live. She had never spent much time with the victims before their demise. Concha did not like the feeling of seeing the cattle that would soon go to slaughter. She got in the Mercedes and waited for her boys to speed her away.

"We are all helping you," Felipe quickly stated after the threesome had left. He sensed that Morgan was shaken by seeing Concha. "We are all working to get you through this fight. That is what it is, not just a game. You must use the match as a vehicle to annihilate Ixma. The game is your only way to get to him. Even so, you have picked up the blocking quickly. I must say, that as my student, you are making me proud," he stated.

"Thank you, O exalted one!" Morgan said with a joking tone in her voice. Morgan got into the old truck and sat back in the seat, closed her eyes and let the cool air of the ocean wash over her face.

"I am getting a bit itchy. I just want to get it over with," Morgan said as she sat up and looked over at Felipe.

"I know Morgan. It is the tension that every warrior feels when they know that they are going into battle. It is a good sign," Felipe said and then turned away. He quickly decided to give her a well-earned compliment." You have been doing an exceptional job of the blocking. You have really learned how to use your mind in the Underworld."

"Thanks. I feel that my focus has improved since we came back from Mexico City. I really am getting the essence of the game." There was a silence for a few moments as Morgan let Felipe take in the meaning of her words. She wanted to say that she had gotten the understanding from Felipe that she needed in the pool in Mexico City. She was at peace now and did not have to wonder about his feelings for her. She felt that she had his love and his passion. That was enough for now. "Felipe is right," Morgan thought to herself as the familiar scenery came into view.

"Keep my eye on the goal. Death to Ixma!" she heard herself burst out loudly. "Wow, she thought, "I am certainly getting into the goddess warrior mode." Morgan had found it interesting that in the last two weeks her body and her mind had become focused on the goal. She had now become like a Spartan warrior, living, eating and sleeping the battle in her mind before it happened. She was surprised how she was able to tuck her feelings for Felipe into a corner of her heart, like a security blanket. They were there if she needed to feel that someone cared about her. Something inside of her had to know that someone wanted her to live.

****
***************************************.

Concha had been resting a great deal during the month of March. "I need to save my strength," she said to herself as the two men helped her out of the car. The last week had forced her lovers to take on the roles of caregivers. When she got through the front door, she went straight to her bed. It did not take her long to slip into the dream state. "Hello, brother," she said to the image of Ixma hovering in her mind. He was very eager to know if Morgan could play the game well. "I have been to her practice. Felipe has taught her well. She has mastered the game."

"I am glad that you have seen her. You could not leave it up to those two fools. They may be good in bed, but do not know how to play the game. Now you must rest as I must do. Stay in your bed until midnight of the 20th. Then get everyone ready for the game. You must come with me to the Underworld. There you will see my victory and feed upon her life force. The Ancestors will watch over the game. The Lords of Night will also revel in my victory. They will roar with delight when I let go of my passion all over her and then suck the life out of her." A hideous laugh was emitted from the fiendish little man. "Sleep well, sister," he said with more laughter and then faded from her mind.

"Yes, I will sleep well, brother," were her last thoughts as she drifted back into the dream state. Whether she had been asleep for hours or minutes, Concha did not know. She suddenly found herself in a rich, green forest. There were trees that she had never seen before. She felt that she was in a strange land. "It is cloudy and overcast in this strange place," Concha thought. "I wonder if this is a real place?" she pondered as she walked along the emerald carpet of moss. Concha walked by trees, ferns and lush bushes. This was not a tropical place, like the Yucatan. It was a cold, verdant forest. Concha kept walking for what seemed like a long time. Then she came to a creek. There were some rocks that acted as stepping stones to the other side.

On the other side of the fast moving water was a woman. The woman looked like she was washing clothes in the fast moving water. She was laundering clothes the old fashioned way, scrubbing them against the rocks to clean them. Concha had seen her mother and other women do this type of washing during the time of her childhood. The woman, whose face peaked out from under long black hair, kept her head down as she pounded the clothes on the rocks.

Concha came to the edge of the creek and realized that the woman was washing the dress she had worn to the recent Christmas dinner. Concha looked at the woman more closely. The woman then lifted her head. She had piercing green eyes. The Washer at the Ford seemed hauntingly sensual. She smiled, but she made Concha anxious. Then the smile turned in to a diabolical, haunting laugh. Concha saw that the water running over her clothing had started to turn a deep scarlet. Suddenly, Concha realized that it was blood gushing out from her dress, turning the water red. The washer women threw her head back and kept laughing louder and louder. The creek was now thick and swollen with crimson blood as it overflowed its banks. The washer woman's laugh was deafening. Concha wanted to leave, but her feet were stuck to the earth. Then she awoke.

"What have I just seen?" she asked herself as she got up from the bed. She hobbled over to a full bottle of Tequila on her dresser. She opened it and drank heartily. When a third of the bottle was gone, she went back to her resting place. Soon the liquor took effect and Concha was able to enter a dreamless sleep.

March 20ᵗʰ

"We are not going to practice today, Morgan. It is time for you to prepare for the battle," Felipe stated when he came into her room after sunset. Felipe had told her yesterday that they would not meet until the early evening. Morgan had been waiting in her cell, meditating and doing Qi Gong all day.

"First we must start with stretching exercises. Then we will do prayers and ceremony. We will do the preparations at my house. You must gather your strength and courage tonight," he declared as he escorted her to his truck.

"I understand what you are saying, Felipe. It all started to 'hit me' today. When I awoke my first thought was of victory, success and triumph," she said as she looked at him with serious, yet hopeful eyes.

"Morgan, we have prepared you as much as possible. You are a good student, a great student," he stated firmly. They arrived at Lupe's home and went through the blue door, the side entrance of the building. This side entrance opened up to another blue door that was Felipe's living quarters. Morgan was astonished when she went inside.

"You have some exquisite, ancient art here, Felipe," Morgan exclaimed as she looked at his spiritual statues that came from all over the world. There were also many candles around the room. It had the air of a temple or holy place. There was a large bed, and antique desk, and lamps. In one corner was an altar to the Virgin of Guadalupe and other goddesses. A table on the other side of the room held crystals, bowls, potted plants and other shamanic tools. The smell of what Morgan knew to be Copal hung heavy in the room.

"I have an extensive collection of goddesses from all over the world. I am very connected to indigenous artifacts," he stated.

"I can feel the energy in here," Morgan said as she acted on Felipe's gesture to sit on one of the large pillows in the center of the room.

"The energy is concentrated in here, Morgan. I have been building this frequency for the last ten days. This is a week in the Mayan calendar that is favorable for you. You are in an empowering week, so this will help you. There is a glass of tea for you on the table. Please drink it. It will put you into a deeply relaxed state for the meditation. We will stay in this state until it is time to get ready. The herbs in the drink will nourish your body and will help you to find clarity during your Underworld stay. "

Morgan did not know how long she had been in the meditative state that the drink had helped her attain. She had not seen any visions, as she usually did when she went into deeper levels of consciousness. When she opened her eyes, she felt deeply rested.

"Stand up, Morgan, "Felipe directed. "We are going to do some stretches. Your body is stiff from sitting. We need to loosen it up." Felipe then stood up and positioned himself across from her.

"Just do what I do" he said. He began to lead Morgan through some stretches that were very similar to Yoga.

"Is this Mayan Yoga?" Morgan asked with a giggle.

"You could say that." He responded with a laugh. "These are stretches that the handball players used to do before a game." After about an hour of stretching, Felipe gestured for Morgan to stop.

"It is now time to get ready, Morgan. I will do a ceremony here, while you are in the Underworld, as an offering to the Lords of Night, the rulers of the Underworld. I am going to ask them to help you. I will beg that they have mercy on you. I will implore them to allow justice to take place and rid the upper world of Ixma and Concha. I feel they need to know why you are fighting this game. It is my plea that they will be compassionate and support you. I will burn Copal and sing the old chants of the Maya. "

"I want to thank you for all that you have done for me, Felipe," Morgan stated. "Felipe," Morgan said again, with the tone of a little girl in her voice, "I know I have a chance to live because of your help. Do you think I will come out of this alive?"

"I know that you were sent here to do this. I recognize that all the forces of creation are on your side. Yes, Morgan I know that you will come back to me." He gave her an emotion-filled look and then left the room. Morgan sunk to her knees and began to pray. "Please help me Mother Mary and Ix Chel," she said as she bent her head. "Please help me and protect me in the Underworld. Four months ago I wouldn't have cared if I lived or died, but now I want to live!"

"Morgan, do not let fear overtake you. Vanquish it from your mind. It has no place with you," she heard in her mind.

"Morrighan?" Morgan said to herself. "Are you here?"

"Yes, my dear. Go put your hands in water and I will infuse you with my strength." Morgan went to the sink in the adjoining bathroom and ran water over her hands. She felt immense energy flowing into her. More than she had ever felt. She was able to feel the passion of battle opening within her. Morgan felt the fervor of those who had come before, those who had fought in the name of the goddess Morrighan. She felt their support. It was as if an army of primordial fighters were now inside her. "You are now full of all that I can give you. Your sister warriors are with you. Their spirits will guide and help you in this battle. Farewell." The Morrighan's voice faded quickly for her mind.

A few minutes later, Felipe came in and was carrying the handball ceremonial gear that she had been using for months. It now smelt different. "Lupe has put many oils on the inside of the protective body armor for you. They will energize you and give you strength. There are many herbs from the South. The Cocoa leaves Lupe used in this blend will give you vitality. I will dress you. Please take all your clothes off and close your eyes. Stand with your legs and arms spread apart."

Morgan disrobed, opened her legs, her arms and closed her eyes. She could feel his hands touching the skin of her abdomen as he put the connecting strip of leather between her legs. He fastened the notched rubber belt where the three parts came together at the base of her spine. "Stay focused on the game, Morgan," she said to herself. Morgan realized that there was something sacred about the ritual of dressing for the handball game. She let herself open to the gathering of power. That thought led to an image of beams of gold light flowing into her outstretched hands and arms. When the belt was in place, he asked her to open her eyes and sit down on the nearby chair. He slowly and carefully put the ceremonial boots on her, one at a time. "Focus, focus," she yelled mentally to herself, as she found herself breathing a bit heavier. Morgan didn't want to look down at her body, so she put her head straight up. She did not want any erotic feelings to pop up at this moment. Even though she was half naked and this was the most he had touched her in the whole time they had been together, she needed to put that aside.

"Please stand up, Morgan and move away from the chair," he said softly. She stood up, moved and kept her eyes closed as she moved. He went behind her and brought the breast plate down over her head. Morgan could feel the thick leather go over her breasts. She took in several deep breaths and big swallows as he tied the leather straps that met behind her back. The touch of his fingers on her back was the closest thing to a caress that she would get from him. She allowed herself to savor it deeply for a few long moments. Felipe did not disturb her. He honored her silence. She was now fully dressed in the female Mayan handball regalia.

After the ceremonial equipment had been placed upon her, Felipe went to a chest of drawers in the corner of the room and took an object out of the bottom drawer. He returned with a narrow item encased in a black cloth, covered in Mayan symbols. It was about eight inches long. "This is an ancient ceremonial Obsidian blade. It is one of the artifacts that my teacher gave me before his death. My master told me that the blade came from the earliest Maya. It was crafted at a very pure time in Mayan history. Therefore the energy that it carries is very intense and yet just. Mother Mary instructed me to give it to you the day that we went to visit her at the church." From between the folds of the mysterious cloth, Felipe withdrew a slim, Obsidian, serrated dagger. The blade of the artifact was a long slender triangle that came to a faultless point.

The handle had leather straps of several faded colors. Morgan had a look of shock on her face as Felipe showed her the chiseled weapon. "This is the exact knife that the women in my vision, at the church in Mexico City, gave to me. It was one of the many scenes I saw when we were kneeling at the church of the Virgin of Guadalupe."

"Really, Morgan?" Felipe replied with an air of curiosity and disbelief in his voice. "She gave you the Obsidian Blade? That is really significant! It means that the Holy Mother is with you. She has shown you the tool of Ixma's ruin. There is no question about it now. I know that that you will succeed in your mission."

"The blade has an interesting smell. Sweat and blood, I think," Morgan said as she rested it in the length of her hand.

"Very astute" Felipe replied. He let her sense it for a few moments. Then he instructed her to grasp it as if she were going to use it. Morgan felt a jolt of heat go through her as the blade made itself at home in the palm of her left hand. She closed her fist around the weapon and her whole arm started to move in ways that what Morgan sensed were attack movements. The impressions she received from the blade, when she closed her eyes, were many. In a few moments, the blade told her all that it had seen and done in the Mayan empire of long ago. Morgan opened her eyes. She was in awe of what she had seen. "There is great enchantment within this blade. It has been used to heal as well as to kill," Morgan stated as a matter of fact.

"Practice holding it and thrusting it." Felipe suggested.

Morgan was fascinated with the blade. She felt mesmerized by it. "I almost feel like I am falling in love with the blade," Morgan stated after a few moments.

"That is a good omen. The blade is connecting with you. The full knowledge of the potential of the blade has been lost. Even my mentor did not know the extent of its abilities. Your day sign is Obsidian Blade. You have a special bond with the dagger because of your Mayan astrology sign. Place the handle of the blade at the end of your breastbone, so that the tip rests in the hollow of your neck. Take in a deep breath and see a circle of your life force going from your mouth, through the point of the blade to its handle. Then see the energy coming back up, through the knife, into your throat. This will bond you to it. It will help the instrument of Ixma's demise to reach its target." After Morgan had been breathing into the weapon for a few minutes, and doing as he instructed, Felipe came over to her. He took the dagger from her.

"I can see the energy fields around you and the blade. You have established your connection. Is the left hand your dominate hand?" He asked.

"Yes. I'm left handed." Morgan stated softly. He then put the Obsidian blade in the outer side of her left boot.

"You will use the dagger at the precise moment. Your aura has embraced the blade and it will serve you at the right time. That is all that I know to say to you. You will sense where to thrust the blade when the moment is at hand. You will know when and where to thrust it."

"Ixma has a weak spot. No one knows where it is on his body. You will be guided to plunge the knife in the correct place at the right time. Mother Mary has told me as much." Then Felipe went to his altar that was obviously dedicated to the Virgin of Guadalupe. He took the gift he had gotten Morgan at the church in Mexico City from the altar. Felipe walked behind her again and put a necklace around her throat. It was the vile of holy water that he had gotten when they went to the church. "I made this pendent for you. It has the love and strength of Mother Mary in it. She will watch over you." At the base of her neck he fastened the little vile that had been laced with silver wire and then attached to a rawhide strap.

"Now you are ready, Morgan." he said. Morgan was naked except for the handball regalia. "Here is a poncho to put around you." Over her head he placed a loosely woven garment. "We must now go to Boca

Negra. Concha will be waiting there for us. She is going to the Underworld with us."

She is probably assuming that she can get puffed up with my life force. NOT HAPPENING!!!." Morgan yelled with determination.

"Good, Morgan, you are getting pumped up for the game. When you see how disgusting Ixma is, that will help your resolve as well," Felipe said forcefully as they made ready to leave. He opened the door and then walked out of the room. As they walked to his truck, Felipe added, "Do not let Concha intimidate you. She is really harmless. It is her brother that is the problem. He will probably present himself in his true form: an obnoxious, rotting dwarf. Do not let his appearance intimidate you or unsettle you. It is very important to understand that, even though I have placed a great deal of emphasis on winning the game, the real goal is to kill Ixma. When you are shown, either during or after the game, where to plunge the dagger, do not hesitate."

Once again, Morgan saw the pathetic structures of Boca Negra come into view. The Mercedes was already in the parking area. That meant Concha was at the portal. This time, when she saw the place, she was filled with many emotions. She was feeling great apprehension about the task before her. Morgan also felt a great sense of awe about the new person that she had become since.

"Well, I am not that whimpering trophy wife that I was when I first came here," Morgan said to Felipe.

He came to a stop in the center of the dilapidated structures. His laugh was hearty and infectious. Soon they were both laughing.

"You certainly are not," he said when they calmed down. "You have become the warrior priestess that you were meant to be. You are ready to embark on your new life. This is the beginning, Morgan, not the end. I know it," he said emphatically and squeezed her hand. By this time it was well past midnight and was March 21st. The dark ocean and the empty fire pit was all that was the same from that night just three months before. He turned to her, took hold of both her hands and turned her to face him. " I will be in my house, sitting in prayer. I will be sending you energy from there. I need to sit in prayer. Stay centered, Morgan. Do not lose your focus, no matter what you may   see,   hear   or   feel."

"Yes," she replied. He let go of her hands and went to the other side of the truck to open her door. The solemn couple left the truck and went to the portal to the Underworld. Morgan saw Concha waiting for her, dressed in her Mayan finery. The portal was now emanating the same sinister, red color she had seen on the Winter Solstice.

"You do not need to take the potion to go through the portal tonight. You must return before sunset tomorrow, on the 22nd of March. Otherwise you cannot return through the portal without the potion." Morgan's eyes widened as Felipe quickly issued this warning. Felipe motioned to Morgan to walk to the Portal. Concha was at the edge, ready to step in.

"Come, my dear." Concha smirked. She also pointed to the revolving wheel of blood orange radiance.

As soon as they stepped into the stone loop, that now emitted a crimson light, she experienced the pressure, the screeching, that was all too familiar. "I am a warrior, now," she said to herself as she hovered over the cross at the handball court of Uxmal. It was her new mantra that she kept repeating over in her mind. She had again come through the portal to the Underworld. Morgan kept repeating another new mantra to herself "Down with Ixma," as she floated on the now familiar playing field of the handball court.

"Welcome, my dear" was the proverbial greeting that Morgan heard from Concha as she sailed away from the cross shaped portal.

"My dear! Is that all she knows how to say?" Morgan asked herself, feeling her verve rise within as her body prepared for the contest. "Good thing she cannot understand a lot of English!" Morgan smiled at Concha and then floated to her side of the court.

The next to appear was Concha's revolting brother, Ixma. He was dressed in the male version of handball attire. He certainly did not look anything like the façade of the sexually potent man that his magical powers could create. His skin was a yellowish color. It had become that way from centuries of no exposure to the light of day. He had no hair. He smiled at Morgan as he floated toward her. She could not help but wince as he showed her his rotting teeth. "Mimi me looked good compared to him!" she muttered.

"Wow, Felipe was right. That guy is nauseating!" Morgan thought to herself as Ixma took his place for the game.

"We waiting for Lords of Night and Ancestors." Concha announced telepathically. The tension of the event and all the herbs that were now speeding through Morgan's body had a fascinating affect upon her. She started to be very agitated and decided to move around a bit before the game started. "I think that I will work off some of this tension." Morgan started to give an acrobatic performance in the air. She zipped around the handball court, doing summersaults and other dance moves. She zoomed from one end of the court to the other. The warrior priestess put on a superb dance performance for the gathering crowd.

By this time there was a menacing, shadowy mist forming around the handball court. When the haze settled, Morgan could make out the silhouettes of men and women wearing Mayan attire. They looked as if they were seated on bleachers in the air, ready to watch the latest entertainment. Concha announced mentally, in English, "Lords of Night and Ancestors here."

"No tension here," Morgan thought. She sensed the emotion coming from the specter- like audience. Morgan felt amusement and interest from the viewers. She also felt the gloomy, sinister disposition of the Lords of Night. After a few more acrobatic displays, Morgan settled down and floated to the center of the handball court, where the magician of Uxmal was waiting.

"Ixma serve first." Morgan heard Concha announce.

Morgan went to the far end of the court, as Felipe had instructed her to do. She was moving back and forth in the air, waiting for the game to begin. After Ixma had served, and the ball came toward her, she approached it with vigor. She sent it flying toward her goal, which was on Ixma's side of the court. During her practices, she had been able to adapt the technique that her grandmother taught her for going into the trees. She was able to stay in one place, hit the ball with her hip, and then see herself going into the ball, pushing it toward her goal. The orb got very close, but Ixma was able to block it.

"Bummer!" Morgan thought to herself, as her attempt to score had been obstructed. This frustration was easy for her opponent to interpret.

Even though Ixma could not understand her language, or Morgan his, he could easily read her emotions. He laughed heartily as he got into position to receive the serve. Morgan could feel the sexual energy that was building inside of Ixma.

Now it was time for Morgan to serve to the magician. "He is not as good as I am," Morgan thought as she watched him approach the ball. She was able to block his attempt to score easily. "I am pumped up!" she thought. She kept doing moves that were a combination of acrobatics and modern dance while waiting for the ball for her serve. Morgan sensed that the Lords of Night were pleased with her and the way that the game was progressing. "I have really gotten the hang of the Underworld thing," Morgan thought. She sensed that the Lords of Night were impressed with her dexterity and grace as she played the game.

Ixma took his turn at defending his goal. Even though she did some fancy moves, Ixma was able to block her attempt to score. When Ixma tried to get the ball through Morgan's circle, she found it easy to obstruct his efforts.

On the third serve that she received, Morgan succeeded in getting the ball past Ixma and through the stone disk. When she scored the goal, she felt a wave of elation come from both Ixma and Concha.

"Why are they so happy? I just scored!" Morgan thought to herself. She looked over at Concha and she was grinning from ear to ear. "Something is wrong here." Morgan reflected while waiting for Ixma to get into position for his serve. "Why are they glad that I got the ball through my ring?" Morgan was beginning to sense that something was amiss. "No one feels good when the opposing team scores. Is this some peculiar Mayan tradition?" she pondered. Morgan was now beginning to feel a mixture of emotions: confusion, fear, and doubt were gushing up within her. She felt as if her thoughts were going millions of miles a second. "What is going on?" she deliberated as the ball came toward her. She didn't have more time to think about it. She had to thwart Ixma's attempt to attain a goal.

"I feel that something odd is going on here, but I can't sense exactly what. I can't stop now. I just have to be on guard," she realized.

Ixma had gotten warmed up, and he was now doing a better job of blocking. Morgan got lost in the game and the disturbing suspicion faded. She felt powerful and forceful as she paraded around the handball court, doing summersaults as she blocked Ixma's attempt to score. She experienced the elation of the audience build with each of her acrobatic displays. Her actions were above and beyond what was needed to play the game.

"Ok, I am going to end this right now," Morgan said to herself. She decided she would use the next serve to win the game. "I only need to score another goal and I will be the winner," she thought. Morgan was now in high gear. If she had not been pumped up before, she was now. She kept bouncing around the court waiting for his serve.

Ixma sensed her new determination and actually smiled his putrid smile and nodded his hairless head at her. Even though he could not understand her thoughts, he was enjoying the energy that she was emitting.

When he served the ball to her, she enacted a daring set of moves that she had perfected during her practices. She hit the ball up in the air above Ixma's circle. Next she went behind her opponent's circle and then slam dunked it downward into his ring.

When the sphere went through Ixma's circle for the second time, everyone was elated: Morgan, Ixma and Concha.

"Why are THEY so happy?" Morgan thought. She was about to find out.

Abruptly she was pressed down to the ground. The warrior priestess was flat on her back. She could not wrestle herself free or resist this force. The elation of her victory was now replaced with a vigilant state of mind. She was again on high alert. She could not free herself from the energy that was holding her down. Then her arms and legs were spread apart. She felt as if there were invisible shackles on her wrists and ankles. The depraved midget let out an unworldly laugh as he came floating towards her. Her handball belt and breast plate were suddenly opened and flew off her body. She was naked except for her boots. Unfortunately, Ixma's handball outfit also flew off his body, revealing the totality of his horrendous physical form.

"Don't struggle, my dear." Concha said in English to Morgan as Ixma floated toward her. He was moving toward her open legs. Morgan could see his extraordinarily large, erect penis coming closer to her.

"Ugh! Gross!!" Morgan thought as she stared at the salami sized erection that was coming toward her.

"Ancient Mayan handball rule, my dear. The winner always offered to gods. Only the best for them!" Concha said in English. The 3,000 year old woman emitted a laugh that would have put The Morrighan to shame.

"DO NOT lose your focus, Morgan," she told herself as the repulsive midget began to float above her pelvis. "The fat lady has not sung yet," she thought. "Where is his weak spot?" she screamed in her head as she remembered Felipe's words. Then Morgan started to see the base of his spine light up. That area was glowing white as Ixma descended over her body. Soon he was hovering directly above her, his penis a few inches away from her wide open legs. "OK. I see where to strike, but how do I get free to deliver the blow?" she implored mentally.

It became obvious that Ixma was going to relieve himself all over Morgan before he sucked the life out of her. Morgan was breathing very hard. She was inhaling and exhaling deeply, revving up her body to strike. "I don't know how I am going to do this, but I am ready. I need to get to the dagger. Focus, Morgan" she told herself. As the nauseating creature, Ixma, made sounds that resembled a man about to have an orgasm, she looked up to the heavens for help. "Someone, please free me! Now is a good time!" she yelled in her mind.

As she mentally screamed her plea, Morgan felt a sense that somehow everything was going to be ok. She had the sense that help was on the way to her. Then Morgan saw a whirling, grey cloud that was rapidly approaching the handball court from behind Ixma.   Concha saw the haze. Morgan sensed Concha's puzzlement. Morgan was able to turn her head to see the Lords of Night laughing and cheering.

Ixma was in the midst of his victory orgasm and did not notice the swirling vapor approaching.   He was hovering a couple of inches above Morgan. As he was about to uncork all over her, the cloud suddenly descended over Ixma. He responded as if a swarm of bees had suddenly come down upon him. He started to swat the murky fog away from his face and body with his hands, but it would not leave him.   The magician of Uxmal started shrieking as his whole body became engulfed in the whirling, sinister mass. He was still floating above her.

The energy that was holding Morgan down suddenly evaporated. Ixma had been distracted enough to let go of his hold on her. Still on her back, she was able to reach her left hand down to her boot as she grabbed the knife from its hiding place. She mentally zeroed in on the space between the anus and penis of his body, which was still suspended above her. She started to take short, quick breaths. Then she closed her eyes and surrendered to the tool of destruction.   As it locked on to the target, a wave of energy overtook her body, making it possible for the sacrificial blade to find its mark. She felt the dagger was moving with some force not her own.

The blow was swift and true. In an instant the blade was thrust in the midget's anus. Then, with the aid of the power surging through her, Morgan swiftly pulled the dagger up the front of his body. Morgan could hear a sound that reminded her of dragging a knife through old, mold-ridden cloth. "Like gutting a fish on Gerard's boat," Morgan mused as she became engulfed in an explosion of energy within her. She knew that the knife in her hand had done its job. His flesh was thin and brittle. It succumbed to the dagger easily.

Morgan had never heard such a horrible scream in her life. She opened her eyes and realized that she had opened up Ixma's body from the base of his spine to his breastbone. Thousands of tiny, round crystals had poured out all over her. The once feared magician of Uxmal was now a lifeless heap of flesh that had fallen on top of Morgan.

"Gross," she though as she pushed the smelly, shriveled tissue off her body. The murky, churning vapor had left Ixma and was now settling in over her. Her first instinct about the fog was that it came to help her. Even so, she tightened her hold on the Obsidian blade. She felt the energy from the knife surround her body. Morgan knew that the blade was creating a protective field around her. She could feel the wrath and frustration within the cloud.

As the thick haze closed in around her, Morgan was able to sense its true nature. She felt the rage and misery of the women's souls that were trapped inside the spinning fog. She experienced their desperation to depart the Underworld. A lucid message came into Morgan's mind as she attuned to the spiraling, shadowy mass: "They are not here to hurt me. They want me to take them out of here. LET'S GO!" Morgan shouted in her mind.

She felt like she was being picked up by a hurricane and carried through the handball court. She was taken to the portal. Then the pressure and the screeching of being transported out of the Underworld swallowed her up. She felt her toes touch the sand of Boca Negra, yet the force that was transporting her did not stop.

All that Morgan knew was that she was out of the Underworld and traveling at an unbelievable speed through the air. In a few moments, she could see a glimpse of the house, that had been her prison for the last three months, come into view. The forbidding miasma had now become a funnel that moved her toward the seaward window of her little room at Concha's home. She felt the souls close in around her, creating a protective cover around her as they burst through the glass window. The grey funnel took her over to the bed where she hovered for a moment. Next, an invisible energy, from outside of the cloud, moved her hand that still held the dagger. This new energy seemed to come from nowhere to Morgan. It plunged the blade into the picture of Gerard that had been turned upside down on the night table. As soon as the dagger went into the picture, Morgan's body was released, and she landed on the bed. She became aware that the cloud, which had transported her, was beginning to evaporate. Morgan felt the fog unwinding from around her body.

Even though her eyes were closed, Morgan could see a bright, white light enter the room. Then the mist and the white light departed and left Morgan to rest in profound solitude and darkness. Morgan could feel the residue of the bliss and joy that the white light embodied.

It was dark when Morgan opened her eyes. She was lying on the bed naked, except for her handball boots and the sticky fluid that was all over her. "Go to the shower and stand in the water," she heard. She took off the boots, got into the shower and propped herself up against a shower wall. She finally felt that the experience was over as she let the water pour over her. In about 15 minutes, Morgan felt as if she was coming back to life. She got out of the shower, dressed and then, for the first time in three months, went out of her room by herself. The guard was gone. She could hear amped up Mexican music coming from the house. She quickly went to the entrance of the adjoining garage. She found the keys to Concha's Mercedes sport coupe hanging on a hook on the wall.

Soon she was on a mission to get to Felipe's house ASAP. It was good that it was the middle of the night. She was going so fast that she would have surely hit someone if it was daytime. The knowledge that she was finally free was beyond exhilarating. It was overwhelming.

She pulled up in front of the blue outside door to Lupe's compound. Morgan burst through that and then she went to the blue door that was the entrance to Felipe's room. She thrust the unlocked door open and found Felipe sitting in meditation. He opened his eyes to see her standing in front of him.

"Morgan, cara mia, you did it!' He stood up to embrace her. She rushed to him and pushed him down on the nearby bed

.

"WHY DIDN'T YOU TELL ME THAT THE WINNER GETS SACRIFICED AFTER THE GAME???" she screamed.

"Morgan, remember that I said…." He could not finish his sentence. Her mouth was on his. Her pent up fervor was finally able to be expressed. Their bodies began to move with a rhythm that seemed to Morgan to be a memory.

Raven

It was just turning light when Morgan left the Malibu house to go to the stable. She accepted that this was the day that she had to face it all. She couldn't wait any longer to ride Raven on the beach again. The long, slow tones from a flute floated out of the upstairs window of the house as she opened the door to the stable. After getting Raven saddled, she decided to mount him, instead of walking him to beach, which was their usual routine. She already knew that reporters would be waiting there for her. The maids had told her that they had been there every day for over a week now. She had been able to ignore them so far. "I have to face them sometime, so now is good. I need to ride Raven again," she thought. She had visited him daily since her return. Morgan could feel his impatience and his love for her. That morning Felipe had told her that today was an empowering day for her. He had said that she would communicate well today.

While she and Raven were ambling toward the trail that led to the beach and the mob of reporters, Morgan wanted to think of something positive and uplifting. She brought into her mind scenes from the three days of lovemaking that started the night she came to Felipe's room. The energy of their bond, his ardor and her receptivity, was unlike any sexual encounter Morgan had experienced in her life. The dreams that Morgan had during those nights showed her that she and Felipe were connecting through their past lives, as well as the present one.   The tie between them was now complete.

The feelings of ecstasy they had shared faded as she and Raven ambled down the trail and the beach came into view. Morgan could hear the voices of the reporters and saw them all come to attention as they saw her come into view. It had been nice that no one expected her to return. When she and Felipe heard about Gerard's death while at Lupe's hacienda, Morgan knew that it would be safe to come back to the states. Felipe translated the reports on Mexican television that said that Gerard died of a heart attack in a hot tub in Vale, Colorado.

Before they arrived in LA, Felipe's sister had helped Morgan get a top notch international probate lawyer.   When Gerard's family had insisted on a prenuptial agreement, Morgan's mother retained a lawyer that got Morgan two billion dollars and her four favorite estates throughout the world. That included the Malibu house. Morgan thought as she walked Raven toward the reporters, "Did mom know this would happen?"

The reporters knew she was alive after the lovers had been at the Malibu house for a couple of days. The staff at the Malibu estate was surprised yet overjoyed to see her. They welcomed her back. All except Esmerelda. Morgan saw the fear in her eyes and fired her the day she returned. The new widow felt that the turncoat employee had brought about the media spectacle.

The reporters were there, on the public beach, with their microphones and cameras, poised to pounce on her. As Morgan and Raven were ambling to the wet sand, she received a message from The Quiet Voice.

"Your new life must be kept secret." she heard clearly.

By this time the reporters were ready to swarm around her. "Mrs. De Armond," the group voice kept saying, "What will you do with the billions you got after Mr. De Armond's death?"

"O'Neil. My name is Morgan O'Neil," she yelled over her shoulder as she and Raven approached the wet sand. Morgan stopped the horse at a point where the water met the land. She turned around in the saddle to look at the gathering of media gathering. The multitude was following at a respectful distance. This was probably due to the fact that Morgan was strolling to the wet sand on the back of an immense, black horse.

"WHAT ARE YOU GOING TO DO WITH THE MONEY, MORGAN?" a booming male voice came out from the crowd.

"SHOP, OF COURSE!" she yelled back. The crowd let out a gigantic roar. As she turned back around in the saddle, away from the cameras, she glanced down at her chest. Just beneath the V of her tee-shirt, she could see the new, tattoo-like mark. It had appeared at the base of her breast bone, the day after she killed Ixma. It was a crescent moon, resting on a small letter N, inside a large letter O. It was the Seal of the House of O'Neil. Morgan sensed that the crescent moon represented the spiritual nature of her clan.

As Morgan looked down at the badge of honor she had earned on the Spring Equinox, she whispered to herself, "And go where I am needed." She nodded her head in resolute agreement as she hit Raven with the reigns. He bolted down the beach. She left the horde of media people behind. Morgan closed her eyes and let the stallion transport her to familiar visions of other worlds and times.

About The Author

My mother told me that I barely made it on to the earth plane. My gestation period kept my mother in bed for 7 months. Many years later I brought through a flame drawing that showed the guides watching over me as I grew inside my mother's womb. I was told early in life that my two Russian grandmothers, who came from the old country, had mystical abilities. Indeed, my grandmother, who died in her sleep, knew a week before that her time arrived.

My spiritual awakening started early. I was going to college in Mexico, where I earned a b.a. degree, when I started having supernatural experiences People showed up on my doorstep for healings and psychic readings. I received my first deck of Tarot cards in Mexico. It was there that my trance channeling started as well.

Throughout the years, my quest for spiritual knowledge and tools for helping humanity has manifested many diverse intuitive and healing abilities. In 2001, when I moved to Sedona, Arizona, the American New Age Mecca, I started to communicate with client's departed loved ones. I would also get urgings from their guides and teachers during my psychic reading. It was here that I also started doing health scans and receiving holistic remedies for clients. I have become certified in three different types of energy work: Reiki, Rising Star Chakra Clearing System and Integrated Energy Therapy for getting the issues out of your tissues. Past Life Regression is another tool I have mastered that brings transformation in the areas of relationship, health and career.

My interest in traditional astrology motivated me to learn about Mayan astrology from deceased Mayan scholar Ian Xel Lundgold. His communications from the realms of spirit inspired me to put into writing the teachings that he shared with me. The Mayan Sacred Count of Days is a memoir of our accomplishments. The Mayan Astrology Handbook documents Ian's system of Mayan astrology.

My latest book takes all the knowledge that I gleaned from writing the first two and weaves it into a fun, yet informative adventure. Now that I have written my first fantasy romance, several fiction story lines keep bubbling up from my subconscious. The Mayan Magician's Kiss is the first installment in the Water Goddess Trilogy. The earth, fire and air trilogies, a Steampunk fantasy romance and a story about a magical amulet are waiting to be birthed.